Pastor Gail –

Stories I Like to Tell

– Book 6 –

Merry Christmas !

TIS
THE SEASON

ALSO BY JERRY PETERSON

Novels
Early's Fall
Early's Winter
The Watch
Rage
Iced
Rubbed Out
The Last Good Man
Capitol Crime

Short story anthologies
The Santa Train
A James Early Christmas
A James Early Christmas II
The Cody & Me Chronicles
Flint Hills Stories
Smoky Mountain Stories
Fireside Stories
A Year of Wonder
Hyper Fiction I
Hyper Fiction II
Hyper Fiction III

Stories I Like to Tell
– Book 6 –

TIS
THE SEASON

JERRY PETERSON

WINDSTAR PRESS

The Legal Stuff

.

DEDICATION

To Marge, my wife and first reader.

To the members of my writers groups, *Tuesdays with Story* and *Stateline Night Writers*, sharp-eyed readers and writers who demand the very best of me in my storytelling and craft of writing.

To a friend and one-time colleague who wishes to remain unnamed.

MIRACLES ABOUND ON A SNOWY CHRISTMAS EVE

It's a lot easier to write about bad people than to depict good ones. The villains get all the best lines, while the heroes come off stiff, even smarmy.

Frank Capra could do it. So can Jerry Peterson, who shows us the good people whose kindness never makes the evening news.

He's a master storyteller. Jerry's got a great eye for detail and a great ear for dialogue, and his prose never lapses into sermon.

The folks who populate the dozen stories in this marvelous collection have had a rough go. The Vietnam vets, the widowers, the folks who live by their wits to scratch out a living are nevertheless always willing to give—a warm place to thaw out, a thermos of stew, a truck and the tires off a car. It's the night before Christmas, after all—but I figure these folks keep Christmas every day.

Why do they do it? Because someone needs help.

"What kind of a God would have taken Thelma, his wife," one character asks, near despair. Turns out the kind who works miracles through kind, loving people.

The collection's first story, and Jerry's avowed favorite—mine, too—is even called "A Night for Miracles." In it, the protagonist of many of Jerry's novels and stories, James Early, rescues a newborn calf from the mother who rejects it, then comes across a young couple and their six-day old baby in a broken-down car in a snow storm.

Like all of Jerry's big-hearted heroes, Early is as resourceful as he is kind.

A close runner-up for me is the story "Bump and the Stranger." Bump Asher's wife is dead and Christmas is "Just another day for work." He's alone, minding his store in the snow storm. Good thing he's there. He feeds a homeless Vietnam vet and lends his truck to a man and his wife, who's about to have a baby and desperately needs to get to the hospital. Bump then fixes the car while they're gone and even replaces the bald tires with new ones from his wife's car.

There's even more to the story, but that would be telling.

Too much? In the hands of a lesser writer, no doubt. But Jerry makes you believe in miracles.

Read these stories. You'll feel a lot better about life.

— Marshall J. Cook, author, teacher, and editor, *Extra Innings*

TIS
THE SEASON

Note: Whenever anyone is in doubt about which book of my Christmas stories they should buy, I put my second collection of James Early stories in their hand. I open it to the first story, "A Night for Miracles." This, I tell them, is my favorite Christmas story. It is, without question, the best I've ever written. And it is. That's why it's the lead story in this new collection.

A Night for Miracles

JAMES EARLY kicked up snow as he ran for a calf being battered by its mother, the cow wanting nothing but to be free of this newborn. He scooped up the small one and, as he did, the cow, a slight, boney Hereford, charged Early. His Newfoundland dog threw himself at her. He bit down on the cow's muzzle and held on as she bellowed. The cow bolted backwards, shaking her head, trying to rid herself of this creature as angry as she.

Early tore off for his horse. He pitched the calf across the roan's shoulders, swung into the saddle, and spurred up the side of the ravine. Early let out a piercing whistle, and his dog unloosed himself from the cow. He raced away, she, blood streaming from her nose, hot after him, churning snow only to give up when the blur of black fur disappeared over the lip of the ravine and into the gloom of the evening.

Fifty, maybe a hundred yards on, Early reined in his horse. He studied the calf that laid before him, patches of frozen afterbirth still clinging to its hair. Early worked a gloved hand over the calf's ribs and legs, feeling for breaks. He rubbed the calf's face. "Malleable little critter, aren'tcha?"

The little Hereford flicked its tongue out in a languid attempt to catch Early's hand, to draw it into its mouth, as if the hand were a teat to be sucked.

"Hungry? Well, we'll getcha home, get some milk in you. Gonna be a cold ride, though, and you're already chilled to the bone."

Early pulled off a glove, freeing his fingers. He twisted around and undid the leather laces of the canvas roll behind his saddle. Early shook the canvas out. He swaddled the calf in it as best he could, the cold of the night making steam of his and his horse's breath as he worked.

Helluva way to spend Christmas Eve, Early thought, riding from haystack, to draw, to grove of scrubby trees, checking cattle, the shadowy presence of his wife with him. But she had died months earlier in an awful accident and he just minutes away. If only he had been faster—

Two yearlings stranded in deep snow broke him out of his mental stew. Early roped first one, then the other and dragged each out to keep them from becoming coyote food. This little calf faced the same fate had not he stumbled on it and its momma.

Some momma that wild one. Early figured get her fat on grass come summer and ship her to the meat packer. Be rid of her.

He rubbed the calf's shoulders. This one he'd have to hand raise because he didn't have a dairy cow to put the calf on.

What are you anyway? Early pulled the calf's tail up and checked. *Uh-huh, a heifer.*

He kneed his horse, and she stepped out for home, the Newfoundland trailing behind, shagging along in the horse's track rather than breaking trail for himself. Sure sign the dog's tired, Early thought as he glanced back. He looked up, too, at the sky swept clean of clouds by a front that had come through the day before, at the moon a shade above the eastern horizon, the moon a coppery yellow, flattened on top as if it had been a ball of buttery dough slapped by a giant.

If Early had to be out, at least it was a nice night—no wind. As his horse plodded on, he watched stars spangle themselves out in the darker regions of the sky. He could navigate by them. As long as he kept Polaris over his right shoulder, he'd eventually come out at home or nearby, striking the county road that would take him there. Half an hour he figured. Surely not much more.

Ahead, in the light of the guardian of the night, Early saw the spidery form of a cottonwood that grew by one of the two never-fail springs on his ranch. A previous owner had cemented rocks around the spring to form a pool, so the cows wouldn't muddy the water when they came in to drink. Early also saw a bulky shape in the tree and, when he neared the spring, the shape launched itself into the night—an owl. By its size, Early guessed a Great Horned or perhaps a Snowy that had come south from Canada to where it might better forage for rodents and rabbits.

Early guided his horse up to the pool and found it as he expected, iced over. He stepped down into the snow. Early hammered the ice with his fist. He broke open a hole and pitched the chunks of frozen water away, and drank first. When Early moved back, mopping the sleeve of his mackinaw across his wet chin and droopy mustache coated with ice, his horse pushed up. She drank long. The dog did not. Instead he satisfied whatever thirst he had with mouthfuls of snow.

Early rubbed his horse's face after she lifted her muzzle from the water. "Road's just over the rise, old girl. We've not far to go."

With that he swung back into the saddle, and the trio pushed on—quartet if you counted the calf. But the calf, stiff from the cold, lolled where it laid across the shoulders of the horse, barely aware of its surroundings. When they topped the rise, tableland stretched before them, snow-covered bluestem pasture on Early's side of the county road, wheat and corn fields on the other, silvery in the moonlight. That road came over from State Seventy-Seven to the east and meandered on to Leonardville—a town of no consequence except to the people who lived there—the only things along the road a couple ranchsteads, three farms, and the Worrisome Creek Baptist Church where Early, on Sunday mornings and Wednesday evenings, sat in a back pew listening to Hubert Arnold preach, the man he liked to call the Great Bear of the Plains. Christmas Eve service, he could be preaching now.

A lone pair of headlights came Early's way from Seventy-Seven. He watched them as his horse walked along, watched them worm their way around two bends, then jerk to the north and go down. Into a ditch? Early wondered. He knew it had to be when he saw billows of steam piling up into the night sky. Early spurred his horse into a gallop. That jarred the calf, but he kept a hand on her back so she couldn't be pitched off. Early hauled up on the reins when he neared his line fence and the ditch on the other side, the ditch that held an old Hudson captive, snow up to the vehicle's hood. He bailed from the saddle, jumped the strands of barbed wire, and plunged down, his chaps knee-deep in the snow. Early wallowed his way to the driver's door and wrenched it open.

In the shadows, he saw two people, a man behind the steering wheel and a woman beyond, she clutching something and whatever it was, it squalled. The man held a hand clamped over his nose, blood discoloring his fingers.

"You all right?" Early asked.

"Busted my beak."

"Your woman got a baby there?"

"Uh-huh."

"Your baby all right, ma'am?"

The woman leaned forward, rocking something in the blanket, shushing at it, cooing to it. "Just scared. I held him tight, kept him from hitting anything."

"You, ma'am, you all right?"

"Think so."

"What you all doing out here?"

The man twisted toward Early. "Going home."

"And that would be?"

"Leonardville."

"Where you comin' from?"

"Manhattan. Mary Elisabet birthed our baby couple days ago at the hospital. They let her out tonight."

Early leaned down. He peered at the man. "You Joe Davidson?"

"Uh-huh. An' my wife."

"Heard you'd had a baby. I'm James Early. You know me. Joe, this isn't the best night to be out and the worst night to be in the ditch."

"Hit something or a tie rod broke. I lost it."

"Not all you lost. That steam? Fella, you busted a radiator. Your car's dead."

"We gotta walk then, huh?"

"Well, maybe not too far. Worrisome church is about a half-mile yon way. Service there tonight, so we ought to be able to get someone to drive you all to your place. First, we got to pack that nose of yours, get that bleeding stopped. Come out here in the moonlight."

Davidson slid off the seat, a big kid in jeans and a short jacket and a fedora that may have seen a lifetime on someone else's head before it came to him, the kid a couple years out of high school.

Early kicked the car door shut to keep inside whatever heat remained. He motioned Davidson to lean against the fender. Early pulled his gloves off and stuffed them in his coat pocket. When his hand came out, it held a bandana. Early bit the hem and tore a strip away, then a second. After he rolled each strip into a bean shape, he lifted Davidson's hand from his nose and studied it as he wiped away as much blood as he could.

"Keep your head up now. This is gonna hurt a bit now." Early pushed one fabric bean into one nostril and the second into the other, Davidson wincing at the touch and the pressure. "You got gloves to keep your hands warm?"

"On the seat by Mary Elisabet," Davidson said, his voice nasally, stuffed.

"Well, you wash your hands clean as you can in the snow, and I'll get your gloves, and your wife and baby."

Early, waving his way through steam and the smell of alcohol anti-freeze boiling away, slogged around to the passenger side of the car, a pre-war job, a coupe. He opened the door and crouched down. "Mary Elisabet, I got my horse on the other side of the fence. How about you and the baby ride, and Joe and me, we'll walk until we can get you someone to take you home?"

The woman—a girl, really, now that Early saw her face more clearly—hugged her child to her chest. "I'm afraid of horses."

"You don't have to be. Molly's about as nice as they come, and she likes women and babies. Come on, let me help you to get out." He caught the girl by the elbow and drew her outside. He reached back in for Davidson's gloves, yellow work gloves like those Early wore around the barn. But when he rode, he wore fleece-lined leather gloves. Anything less in the cold was begging for trouble.

"You got gloves, ma'am?"

The girl shivered, giving Early his answer. "Well, here," he said, "take mine."

He stripped his gloves off and snugged the girl's hands into them.

Early started away, going ahead, kicking and tramping through the deep snow, breaking a path for the girl, but she called him back. "We got a suitcase in the backseat," she said. "It's got some things for the baby and a menorah."

"We could leave that and get it tomorrow."

"No, it's important."

"Well, all right." Early chewed at his mustache as he worked his way around the girl to the door. He opened it, pulled the front seatback forward, and reached in for a pasteboard suitcase. Next to it, Early found something far more valuable—a blanket. He pulled both out, banged the car door shut, and went on around the front of the crippled car and up to the fence line, the Davidsons struggling along behind him.

He set the suitcase and blanket over, in the snow on the other side.

Hands free, Early pushed the top strand of barbed wire down. "Joe, you step across, and I'll hand your wife over, all right?"

"Yeah, I can do that."

Davidson eased over the wire. When he turned back, Early swept the girl and her child up in his arms. He passed them across to Davidson, but the hem of the girl's dress snagged on a barb and ripped.

"Whoa up." Early caught the fabric. He pulled it free of the fence and followed across, swinging first one leg over the wire, then the other. Early, with the suitcase and blanket, and Davidson, carrying his wife and baby, pushed on through the snow to where Early's horse stood waiting, the Newfoundland lying nearby.

Early peered at the calf already on the horse and all the cargo he wanted to put up there. "Not sure how we're going to do this," he said to Davidson.

"What's in the canvas?"

"Newborn calf. Her momma didn't want her. Help your wife up in the saddle, would you?"

Davidson moved up beside the horse. He slipped Mary Elisabet's foot in a stirrup and helped her lever up, she holding her child tight—helped Mary Elisabet to sit side saddle.

"I don't like this," she said as she settled on the seat.

"Hon, you'll be all right."

Early held the blanket out to Davidson. "She's gonna be cold up there. What say you wrap her in this?"

"Yeah, that's good." The kid flapped the blanket open. He lifted it at the midpoint of the long side up over his wife's head.

Early moved around to the other side of his horse. He caught an end of the blanket and, working with Davidson, tucked it around the saddle and brought the end forward, up and around the baby and the canvas-swaddled calf.

Early's hands felt the bite of the cold. He thrust them deep into his coat pockets and hustled forward. Davidson, toting the suitcase, came up the other side. The two met and moved along. And the horse followed, but the Newfoundland, instead of trailing behind, jumped out. He broke a trail of his own beside Early.

"Miracle for us you were out here," Davidson said.

"Some of us believe Christmas Eve is a night for miracles."

"I guess."

"Your wife says you got a menorah in your suitcase. I'm thinking that means you're not Presbyterian."

"Jewish, both of us." Davidson gazed down at the snow he kicked before him. "Tonight's the first night of Hanukkah. Took the menorah to the hospital so we could celebrate, you know, light the servant candle and the first candle if they didn't let Mary

Elisabet and the baby out, then they did. Know about Hanukkah?"

"A little."

"The rabbi says it's one of our lesser holidays, but I like to think it rates right up there with your Christmas. It's a freedom thing."

"How's that?" Early asked.

"Couple thousand years ago, fella named Mattathias and his boy led a revolt so we Jews could worship our God, and they won."

"Your temple, wasn't it destroyed in that war? Seems I remember that."

Davidson chuckled. "You do know something of us."

"Sometimes Herschel Weichselbaum and I sit in the back of his store. We visit, and he takes it on himself to make this poor Gentile knowledgeable on a thing or two."

"Mister Weichselbaum's good at that. So he told you we rebuilt the temple?"

"That he did."

"Yeah, had to be some big effort. Mattathias dedicated the temple to God, and that first night he lit a lamp." Davidson smiled as he slogged along. Early wondered if it might be a memory.

"A miracle," Davidson said.

"The lamp?"

"Yeah. See, it burned 'round the clock for eight days, only our people had little enough oil to keep it going but that first night. Mister Early, Mary Elisabet and me, we wanted to celebrate that miracle, celebrate it at home now that we got a baby."

"Boy or girl?" Early asked, pushing along.

"Boy."

"Give him a name?"

"Christofer we're thinking, after my granddad."

"'At's a good name."

"Uh-huh, Christofer Davidson. Custom is to hand the generations down in my family. My granddad says we go back to early Israel days—the House of David."

"That is something. We Earlys hardly track back to yesterday."

"Family history is real important, my granddad says."

"My granddad never talked much of his life and nothing of his parents or brothers and sisters, if he had any. We can date him to the Civil War."

"How's that?"

"He rode with the First Nebraska Cavalry. My dad found a diary from that time tucked away in a trunk."

They came up on a rise and a gate in the line fence. Early opened the gate. He motioned for Davidson to lead his horse and her burdens through, out onto the county road. In the minutes Early had his hands out of his pockets, the cold made his fingers ache. He fumbled the gate closed. When he caught up, he looked up to Mary Elisabet. "Missus Davidson, you and the baby doing all right up there?"

"As long as I keep a hand on the saddle horn."

"Well, the Worrisome church is down there by the creek. Lights are on, so people are still there."

They set out again, easier going walking in tire tracks, the only sound the creak of saddle leather and the crunch of snow under boots. And then they heard it—singing to the accompaniment of an old reed pump organ...

> *It came upon a midnight clear*
> *that glorious song of old*
> *of angels bending near the earth...*

"Pretty, isn't it?" Early said.

Davidson nodded his agreement. "We won't be intruding, will we?"

"Door's open to everybody."

The straggly parade turned off at the driveway and made their way to the stoop. Early climbed the steps, stomping the snow from his boots as he went. When he opened the door, a rush of warmth and the smell of a cedar Christmas tree engulfed him, but no one sat in the pews and no one stood in the pulpit. Yet the singing continued...

> *Peace on the Earth*
> *good will to men*
> *all Heaven and nature sing...*

He turned back, eyeing Davidson and the girl. "Not a soul in there. Tell you one thing, we're all gonna get inside out of this cold. We'll figure it out later. Get your wife, Joe."

Davidson helped Mary Elisabet out of the saddle and into his arms. He worked his way up the steps and inside as Early pulled the calf off his horse's shoulders. He cradled the calf and its canvas wrapper and went on up the steps, his dog shagging behind him. After the Newfoundland cleared the door, Early reached back. He pulled the door closed.

The Rural Electric's lines had not yet reached the Worrisome church, so kerosene lamps illuminated the dozen or so pews and the front, the platform on which stood a wooden manger near the coal stove that warmed the building and, to the far side, a cedar tree decorated with strings of popcorn and chains of yellow and red loops made from construction paper. At the top of the tree resided a cardboard star wrapped imperfectly in aluminum foil.

The tree did not interest Early. He pushed up to the manger and deposited his calf there, in the straw. He worked the canvas loose so the heat from the stove could get to the calf's hair and skin, the calf so cold Early felt she was less than an hour away from death if he didn't get her warm. He rubbed and massaged the calf, working the heat into her body.

Near the manger stood a metal folding chair. Davidson hooked a foot around it and drew the chair closer. He lowered his wife onto it. "Feels some better already, doesn't it?" he said as he helped her open the blanket with which she had wrapped her child.

Mary Elisabet, smiling, gazed at the face of her boy. "Surprising he hasn't cried, what with all that's happened."

"You may have one of those peaceful babies, ma'am," Early said, "let you sleep through the night."

"You have children, Mister Early?"

"Little girl, about three months old."

"That's nice."

"Yeah, it is." He rubbed the calf more briskly.

Early's Newfoundland nosed in. He peered first at the calf, then the baby. As if he were satisfied that all was well, the dog flopped down on the platform midway between the two.

"The people?" Davidson asked.

"All the cars and trucks out there in the side yard, they can't have gone home." Early looked up from the calf, his attention drawn by the sound of cooing—Mary Elisabet cooing to her child, the baby with his eyes open, waving a tight fist at the air around him. "Joe, looks like your family's all right."

From behind, at the far end of the church, the door swung open, and lyrics of another carol rolled in...

We three kings of Orient are
bearing gifts we travel afar...

Early twisted around in time to see a burly man in a great coat and an earlapper cap lead a cluster of people inside—the man, Hubert Arnold. They all stopped and gazed at the manger scene, surprise on the faces of some, awe on others.

Arnold waved a hand toward the mother and child, the calf—alert now—the dog, Davidson, and Early, moisture dripping from Early's mustache as the last of the ice melted away. "Don't this just look like Christmas in Bethlehem."

"Where you been, Bear?" Early asked.

"Out back, all of us, singing to the Christmas star. Cactus, looks to me like Jesus sent you and your menagerie of friends and livestock to complete our manger scene."

"Just trying to get warm. Hadn't thought about it."

One of the women peered around the preacher. "Is that a baby?"

"Oh my lands, it is," another said. She pushed past Arnold. So did a half-dozen other ranch wives. They hustled up the aisle to the platform and clustered around Mary Elisabet and the baby, leaning in, admiring.

One of them took hold of the child's tiny fist. "Isn't she just the prettiest?"

Mary Elisabet gazed down at her child's face. "She's a he. My baby's a boy."

"How old is he?"

"Six days."

Arnold made his way up to Early. "Bet we could rustle you and your friends up some gifts you all would appreciate on a cold night like this."

"Bear, that isn't necessary."

"It is in God's house. It's Christmas. The wife's got a thermos of hot chocolate, a couple here've brought cookies, and I know in my pocket I've got some terrific divinity candy I'm dying to share."

EARLY SAT on the edge of the platform, his hat on the floor between his feet, his dog lying beside him. Early stroked the great Newfoundland's face.

"Bear," he said as Arnold, in the first pew, chewed on a piece of divinity candy, "sure does get quiet when everybody goes home, doesn't it?"

The preacher picked out another piece of candy. "Quiet's good for the soul. Lets one commune with God. You been doing that?"

Early shook his head.

"You thinking about Thelma again?"

Early didn't respond, neither did he lift his gaze from his dog. He just continued stroking the Newfoundland's muzzle.

"Cactus, her death wasn't your fault, you know."

"Sometimes I just get so hateful." Early's words came with a raspiness. "What kind of a god is it that would take her?"

"One who would give you a better gift. Cactus, God gave you Thelma's child—your child. Like the Christmas child, your little girl is the best gift you could have."

Early looked up, the mellow light of a low-burning kerosene lantern reflecting in the wet of his eyes. "Yeah," he said, "she surely is that, isn't she?"

Note: You're going to like Bump. He's a very special man. If, as you're reading this story, you wonder where this story is set, it's set in Strawberry Plains, Tennessee, just a bit east of Knoxville. The time? Sometime before cellphones came into common use. No one in this story has one.

Bump and the Stranger

BUMP ASHER sat in his gas station on a frigid Christmas Eve afternoon. He hadn't been anywhere in years, not since his wife had died. He had no decorations at the house or here—no tree, no lights, nothing to add any cheer to either place. To the old garage man, this was just another day for work.

It wasn't that Bump hated Christmas. He didn't. It was just that without Dixie, his wife of a third of a century, he couldn't find a reason to celebrate. And they had had no children, so indeed he was alone.

He sat there on the edge of his smudged and oil-stained desk, the office redolent with the smell of gear grease and strong coffee. Bump gazed out through the plate-glass window at the snow that had been falling for the last hour, wondering if maybe he shouldn't turn the OPEN sign over and go home. But someone shuffled out of the gathering gloom and into the light of his gas pumps, a man with his hands stuffed deep in his pockets, his back hunched against the weather.

Kind of raggedy, Bump thought. Could he be one of those bums that had drifted down from Knoxville, one of those homeless fellows, as the preacher called them, living under the bridge at the other side of town? Could be.

The man came to the station door. He opened it and stepped inside, stamping the snow from the cracked leather of his shoes. "Mind if I warm myself for a minute, mister?"

"I was about to close," Bump said, not stirring from his seat on the edge of the desk, his arms folded across his chest. "There's a chair there by the space heater. Go ahead and sit a spell."

The stranger bobbed his head. He drifted over to the heater and held his hands out. He warmed them, rubbing them, massaging in the heat radiating from the kerosene burner.

There was something about the man's jacket. Faded and patched as it was, there on the back, Bump was sure of it, was a faint outline of South Vietnam and words stitches in a half-moon above it. What did they say? Thirty-Seventh Hellraisers, Tan-Wo? He hadn't seen a jacket like that in decades. "You in Nam?"

"That and a lot of other places," the stranger said.

"Army?"

The man shrugged, his longish hair, in need of a wash, dripping melting snow.

"Yeah, me, too," Bump said. "Long time ago. Where you livin'?"

"Here and there."

"Kinda understand." Asher picked up the large-mouth thermos from beside him. He screwed off the cap. "Friend, you look like you need a little something in your belly. Try this. Stew. Hot and tasty if I do say so myself. Made it this morning."

The stranger attempted a smile as he accepted the thermos, then sat and sipped at the thick broth.

"Easier with a spoon," Bump said. He leaned back and took a large spoon from the open center drawer of his desk. He tossed it to the man.

At that moment, the driveway bell dinged. Bump glanced up to see a 'Forty-Nine Ford coupe at his pumps, steam rolling out through the car's bullet-nosed grill. "My Lordy, would you look at that antique. Guess I better get out there and see what the driver wants."

At the door, he turned back. "When you're finished with that stew, you help yourself to some coffee on the hotplate. It's fresh."

Bump didn't wait for a response, but trotted out into the late afternoon, to the car, to the window open on the driver side. He leaned down. "You got troubles here?"

"Yes, mister, can you help us?"

Asher saw panic in the young man's face. What was that accent, Spanish? Mexican? Puerto Rican?

"My wife is about to have a baby. I got to get her to the hospital and my car's broken."

"Well, let me take a look. Pull the hood release." Bump pushed back from the door. He moved around to the front of the car and fitted the fingers of his mittened hand into the slot between the top of the grill and the hood. He felt for the paddle release that would pop the hood up, found it, and squeezed his fingers against the paddle until he heard a sproing. Then Bump lifted. He shoved the front of the hood up and out of the way. Steam billowed out, wreathing Bump's face, fogging his glasses, and filling his nose with the stink of boiling coolant.

The garage man pulled a hanky from his back pocket. He dried his glasses and, after he got the bows hooked back over his ears, he peered into the engine compartment. *Aww jeez, block must be cracked.*

Bump leaned around the hood. "Son, you ain't goin' anywhere in this thing."

"But mister—"

"Son, your car's dead." He turned away and went back to the station.

"But mister, I need help."

Bump waved and went on inside, to a board that hung on the wall behind his desk, next to the AC Delco calendar. He took down the keys to his old Dodge truck, twenty years newer than the steaming car at the pumps, but still old. Bump moved on into the service bay where he kept his truck when he had no vehicles to work on. He ran up the overhead door, fired up the Dodge, and backed it out to where the young couple stood huddled next to their expired car.

"Take my truck," he said as he got out. "She ain't the best thing you ever looked at, but she'll get you to the hospital."

"I don't know, mister."

"It's this or walk. I don't think I can get a taxi out here."

"All right then. I got a little money."

"You keep it. You're gonna be needin' it."

"Well, thank you."

Bump shrugged. He turned to the young woman who, from her size, looked like she had all her possessions stuffed up under her coat. "Come on, missy," he said, "let me give you a hand." He guided her around to the passenger side and helped her step up and in while the husband pushed a suitcase in from the driver's side of the cab.

"You know where the hospital is now, don'tcha?"

The husband got in and yanked the driver's door shut. "Yes, mister. You're a savior."

"Aw, not really. You just drive careful. It's slick out there—and I'll call ahead to tell the hospital to expect you." He pushed the passenger door closed. Bump stepped back and watched the couple and the truck roll away out the drive, turn onto the street, and speed off.

"Well," he said to the spirits of the evening. He turned away, back to the service bay. Inside, he called to the stranger as he went on into the office, "Glad I loaned 'em the truck. Fella, you should see the tires on their car. They're shot, too."

But the stranger was gone. There on the desk stood the thermos—empty—and beside it a used styrofoam coffee cup.

The garage man rubbed at the short gray hair on the back of his neck. *Well, at least he got something in his belly.*

Finding himself with nothing to do and no one to talk to, Bump Asher went back outside, figuring he might see whether the wreck of a Ford would start. The driver had left the key in the ignition. Bump twisted the key and held it as the engine cranked. He pumped on the accelerator, squirting more gasoline into the carburetor. That wealth of gas shot into each cylinder on successive downstrokes and ignited.

The engine roared to life.

Bump listened to the engine as he continued pumping on the accelerator. He shifted the transmission into first gear, eased out the clutch, and car rolled away from the pumps. Bump guided the coupe into the open service bay where he stopped it and turned off the motor.

The old girl ain't so dead after all.

He slipped out from behind the steering wheel. Bump pulled the service bay door down, then took a trouble light and leaned across the fender to inspect the driver's side of the engine. If the block was indeed cracked—

But no water leaked from there, nor from the right side of the motor—the passenger's side.

Bump Asher used the hook at the end of the trouble light as a scratcher. He worked it over a sideburn as he moved around front.

That's when he saw it, water puddling beneath the radiator.

The garage man got down on one knee. He peered more closely. There was a drip there, a pretty good drip. He reached up underneath for the hose coming out at the bottom of the radiator. Felt it, spongy and wet.

Shoot. Ahh well, at least it's an easy fix.

The garage man pushed back up. He rubbed at his knee. Arthritis and a cold concrete floor, not a good combination. Bump forced his knee to work as he went over to a wall where an assortment of hoses and V-belts hung. He hummed as he looked them over and took one hose down. *Yeah, that's the right one.*

Asher drained the radiator. When he had that done, he changed out the old, rotted radiator hose for the new one. Not a bad job. Bump flushed the radiator and refilled it with new coolant. He studied the new hose, saw that it held. Not a drop leaked out from anywhere.

Next he examined the car's tires. He ran a hand over the tread of the first, then the next and the next, all as bald as a baby's bottom Bump's father would have said. *These sure aren't gonna get 'em through the winter.*

To the side, in the next bay, resided Dixie Asher's old Lincoln, the model with the suicide doors, the sucker longer than Bump's pickup. He kept the Lincoln parked there, tires like new. He didn't need the car, only drove it enough to keep the battery up, but Bump just couldn't part with the old boat because Dixie had loved it so.

So he ran the Lincoln up on the hoist, and the Ford, too, each enough that he could hit their wheels' stud bolts with an air wrench without having to bend over. Bump went about swapping the wheels and tires from one car to the other. He hadn't quite finished when he heard what sounded for certain like a backfire.

Bump leaned into the office, to peer out through the plate-glass window. A county cruiser idled by his pumps and—

The air wrench dropped from Bump's hand. He bolted for the office door, yanked it open, and ran outside to a deputy lying by the cruiser, the snow crimson at the man's shoulder.

"Charlie?" Bump called out as he went down on his knees beside the officer, the officer hatless.

Charlie Debbs coughed against the cold and the pain. "Bump?" he whispered.

"Yeah. Gawddamn, what the hell happened to you?"

"Shot . . . gotta help me."

"That's for damn sure." Asher got one arm under Debbs' knees and the other under the deputy's shoulders. He lifted and pushed up with his legs, his arthritic knee near buckling under the strain. But it held and Bump shuffled with his burden through the snow toward the office. Turning, he backed through the doorway, using his butt to keep the door open. Inside, he turned again and lowered Debbs onto a ragged overstuffed chair he kept for people who waited while he worked on their cars and pickups.

"Blood's gonna get all over," the deputy wheezed.

"Maybe, but who's to notice?"

Bump's mind raced back over the medic training he'd had all those decades ago. *Pressure, pressure, yeah, that's it. That stops the bleeding.*

The laundry company that serviced his station had been there that morning, and the route man had left a stack of clean shop towels. Bump ran out into the service bay. He grabbed up a handful and a roll of duct tape, and ran back. Bump tore the shoulder of Debbs' uniform jacket open, the jacket reeking of cigarette smoke. He ripped away the shoulder of the shirt as well, to get at the wound. With the shop cloths and the tape, Bump bound the wound, smiling at Debbs as he worked. "They say duct tape can fix anything. You hurtin', buddy?"

"Yeah."

"Think I got something." From his jacket pocket, Bump produced a bottle of pain pills the doctor had given him for his back.

"These'll do ya," he said as he shook a half-dozen into Debbs' hand. Bump got a cup of water and held it to the deputy's lips as Debbs swallowed pill after pill. "Hard work I know, but you hang in there. I'll getcha an ambulance out here."

Telephone . . . call . . . Bump slapped the side of his face. "I was supposed to call the hospital."

He fumbled with the receiver. When he got it to his ear, he heard only silence—no dial tone. "Charlie, line must be out. S'pose I could get one of your buddies on the radio in your car?"

Debbs coughed hard, creating for himself a new wave of pain. He winced and clutched at his shoulder. "You'll get the dispatcher."

"Who's on tonight?"

"Gracie."

"Then we're home safe." Bump trooped outside only to find that a bullet had gone into the cruiser's dashboard, destroying the police radio. He trudged back. "Charlie boy, we're in a helluva fix. Your radio's gone."

"Maybe I can drive," Debbs said. He coughed again, his head racheting forward with the force of it, as he tried to get up. He fell back into the chair, and Bump held him down.

The deputy wheezed, his hand going to his shoulder. "Guess I'm not going anywhere, am I? Thanks for not leaving me out there."

"Hey, buddy boy, what are friends for?"

"Guy that shot me, he's still got to be around. He's on foot."

"That's as may be, but I tell ya, he's the least of our worries." Bump dragged over one of his folding chairs and sat in front of Debbs. There he peeled back the bandage, lifting his head so he could squint through the bottom part of his tri-focals. "Bleeding's pretty well stopped, Charlie boy."

Bump prodded at the wound. "Looks a helluva lot worse than it is. Bullet passed right through the fat of your shoulder. If it hit any bone, it only nicked it. Can't feel anything shattered. Charlie, old buddy, if

I was a bettin' man, I'd bet your pay you're gonna be all right in a month or two. Whaddaya say to a cup of my coffee?"

Debbs shook his head.

"Best in town and you know it. Too bad I don't have any donuts."

The deputy laughed. He twisted, his face creased with pain. "Always the donut jokes. You know I'm diabetic."

"Yeah, I do."

The outside door burst open. In ran a wild-eyed youth in faded jeans and a denim jacket, waving a pistol. "Gimme your cash! I gotta have your cash!"

Bump twisted around to the kid. He saw the boy's hand shaking. "Whoa there, fella. I don't want you shootin' out any of my glass, and I sure don't want you shootin' me."

"Come on, money!"

The deputy touched Bump's hand. "He's the one."

"I figured."

The kid turned more toward the wounded Debbs, but before the kid could do anything, Bump came out of his chair. He stood between the two. "Son, you need to put that cannon away. I got money in my pocket, so you back off a bit."

"Want the money from your cash register, too." The boy waved his pistol at the ancient manual NCR machine on Bump Asher's desk, the back of the cash register papered over with business cards anyone who came through Bump's station always left.

"Oh, I'm sorry about that," the garage man said.

"Why?"

"I already made my bank deposit for the day. All you're gonna get is my walking-around money."

"How much?"

Bump eased his hand into the pocket of his blue twill trousers. When he brought his hand out, it held three bills—two twenties and a five. Bump heard the deputy move behind him. He glanced back as Debbs' hand moved toward his holster and the Glock it contained. The garage man reached back. "Charlie, you leave that. We already got one gun too many out as it is."

Bump turned his focus on the young man. "Son, it's Christmas Eve. You take the money. Just put that pistol away."

He held out the bills. As he gave them over, Bump also reached for the barrel of the gun. He got hold of it.

The kid, his eyes tearing up, released his grip on the weapon. He fell to his knees, sobbing.

Bump gazed at him. "Not too good at bein' a bad man, are ya?"

"All I wanted was to buy something for my wife and little boy," the kid blubbered between sobs. "Lost my job, my car. Behind on the damn rent."

Bump passed the gun, a Smith & Wesson, to Debbs. "Son, we all get in a bit of squeeze now and then. Take it from an old man who's been there, but we make it through the best we can."

He reached down. Bump caught the kid by the arm and helped him up into a chair. He filled a clean styrofoam cup with coffee. "You know," he said, pressing the cup into the kid's hand, "sometimes we do stupid things. Being stupid, that's what makes us human, and you comin' in here with a gun, let me tell you that was stupid. Suppose we see if we can get this thing sorted out."

The young man mopped at his tears and rubbed the sleeve of his jacket at his dripping nose. He glanced over at the deputy. "I'm sorry. I'm sorry I shot you."

"Oh, shut up and drink your damn coffee."

Bump twisted toward Debbs, his eyes wide in surprise.

SIRENS CAME wailing up the street, two of them. A city police cruiser and a box on wheels—an ambulance—swung into the gas station, both skidding in the snow. A patrolman bailed out of the cruiser. He came on the run, gun drawn, through the station's door.

"Charlie, you all right?" he called to Debbs.

"Yeah, but I've had better days. . . . How'd you find me?"

"GPS locator went off in your car. When your dispatcher couldn't raise you, she called me to get out here. What happened?"

"Got shot."

The patrolman, Diz Walker—short and wiry— moved toward the kid, the only one in the gas station office he didn't know. "He the one who did this?"

"Naw. Guy ran off in the dark."

Bump and the young man glanced at one another.

"Dropped his gun, though." Debbs held the kid's weapon out, butt first.

"Gawd, Charlie, you handle this, did ya?" Walker asked. "We won't be able to get any prints other than yours off it."

"Well, I wasn't thinking too clear."

Two paramedics pushed in. Bump knew them, Alice Goodhue and Jeff McKnight. He motioned them toward Debbs, and they, without exchanging so much as a word, went to work cleaning and rebandaging the deputy's wound.

Walker waved his pistol at the kid. "Who's this guy?"

"Works here," Debbs said.

Bump grinned. "Hired him this morning. Fella lost his job, and I'm gettin' a little too old to be working as a mechanic."

The patrolman holstered his pistol, a Glock like the deputy's. "Hell you say. Bump, you'll never quit. Who's gonna take care of my car if you do?"

"The kid here."

Finished, Goodhue and McKnight helped Debbs up. They moved him toward the door and their ambulance, all the lights still flashing. The young man reached out for Debbs' coat sleeve as the deputy went by. "Why?" he whispered.

Debbs stared at him. "It's Christmas," he said.

SOME SEVERAL minutes later, the ambulance pulled away and the city cruiser behind it. Bump Asher put a hand on the young man's shoulder. "Son, looks like you got one doozy of a break tonight. That ought to solve some of your problems, and I think maybe I can help you with one or two others."

He went into the back room where he rummaged around the storage shelves. When he returned, he carried a cardboard box a bit larger than a whiskey case. Bump pawed inside it until he turned up what he was looking for—a ring box that fit in the palm of one's hand.

"Here you go," he said. "Something for your wife. I don't think my Dixie would mind. She told me the day she was dying that someday it would come in handy."

The young man took the ring box. With unsteady fingers, he opened it. There in the velvet lining resided a modest gold band set with a crystal clear stone. The young man stared at Bump. "A diamond?"

"It isn't very big. Didn't have much money back when we got married."

"I can't take this. It means something to you."

Bump pushed the ring box back when the young man tried to return it. "Now it means something to you. I got my memories. That's enough."

He again reached into the big box. This time Bump brought out a Texaco tanker truck. "You say you got a boy, huh?"

"Yeah, five years old."

"Seems I remember boys like trucks. The oil company gave me a bunch of these last year to sell. Last one. Take it for your boy."

Tears again filled the young man's eyes. He mopped at them, then held out Bump Asher's folded money. "I can't take this."

"Now I'd like to know why the hell not? What are you gonna buy Christmas dinner with? Just count it as part of your first week's pay."

"You really giving me a job?"

"Didn't you hear me tell old Diz I need a mechanic?"

"Really?"

"Really. You know what a wrench is and a sparkplug, don't you?"

"Yeah."

"That's enough for a start. You better get on home to your family."

The kid rose. He moved toward the door, but turned back. "I'll be here in the morning—for work."

"Make it the day after. I don't open on Christmas."

Bump watched the door close and, through his station's plate-glass window, he watched the kid hustle away into falling snow and the darkening night, the rear end of the toy tanker truck sticking out from beneath his arm. When Bump turned back, the stranger was sitting at his desk. "Where'd you come from? I thought you left."

"I've been here. I've always been here." The corners of the stranger's mouth drew up in a smile.

"Man, I sure didn't see you."

"Bump—you don't mind if I call you Bump, do you?"

"That's kinda my name. I tell ya, fella, I'm gonna sit down. I'm pooped. It's been a gawd-awful long day."

The stranger stood. He waved Bump to the chair. "You say you don't celebrate Christmas. Why is that?"

Comfortable at last, Bump filled a chipped china mug with coffee, the mug emblazoned with a Crescent wrench and the slogan, 'World's greatest mechanic.' After he stopped pouring, he held the pot over the cup the stranger had used.

"No, thanks. What you gave me before was plenty."

The old garage man set the pot back on the hotplate. "Christmas?" he asked. "Well, after my Dixie died, I just couldn't see what all the bother was worth. Puttin' up a tree, baking cookies like I used to with Dixie. Just wasn't the same by myself."

Asher shook some sugar into his coffee. He stirred the brew with a pencil.

The stranger touched the garage man's shoulder. "Bump, what you do is Christmas. You gave me something to eat and drink when I was hungry, and warmed me when I was cold. That pregnant woman on the way to the hospital, you remember her?"

"Sure."

"She's already given birth to a son who will grow up to be a physician, a healer."

Bump smiled at that.

"The deputy you helped, your friend? A day's coming when he will save the lives of a dozen people who would otherwise die in a bridge washout. And that young man who tried to rob you, years after you're gone he will become a wealthy man, and he will share that wealth with tens of thousands of people. All this is the spirit of the season, Bump, and you keep it as good as any man."

The garage man arched an eyebrow. He glanced up, to better study the face of this person who stood beside him. "You sure you haven't been nippin' at a bottle of Jim Beam?"

The stranger shook his head.

"So how do you know all this, if you don't mind me asking?"

"Let's just say I've got an inside track on this sort of thing." The stranger started toward the door, but he too, like the young man before him, turned back. "I should tell you one more thing."

Bump took his pencil from his coffee. He sucked the drops off.

"There will come a time, my friend, and it's not far off, you're going to see your Dixie. You're going to be with her." The stranger backed away toward the door. "I'd like to stay longer, but I can't."

The garage man sipped from his mug. "Why's that?" he asked.

"I have to be getting home. My father's planned a big celebration."

"Oh?"

"You see, tomorrow's my birthday."

"Well, um, happy birthday then."

The stranger left.

Bump, as he rubbed a finger around the rim of his mug, watched the man in the faded Vietnam war jacket disappear into the snow and the night. He glanced down at his coffee, then back up. *Was there a radiance about him?*

Note: A word of warning, dear reader. This Christmas story is a story of men who have been to war, scarred men, veterans of Vietnam, World War II, and The Great War—World War I. Their language can be and at times is rough, but that's the way they talk. If that makes you uncomfortable, then skip ahead to "Christmas at My House." But if you do, you're going to miss a sterling story.

The Search for Pooch

"SANTA, my boy Charlie wants to ax you somethin'. He won't tell me what it is."

Pappy Brown—Santa Claus for the Tau Upsilon/Theta Delta Theta's Big Brother/Big Sister Christmas party—glanced up at the woman, overweight and frayed. He winked at her, then beckoned to the boy hanging onto the hand of his assistant, six-foot-four elf Junior Dempsey.

The boy, in jeans and a shirt, both well-worn but as clean as if they had just come out of the washer, came away. Pappy caught him under the arms and lifted him onto his lap. "You're about six, aren't you, Charlie?"

"Yes."

"I'm thinking you're wanting to ask me something. What is it?"

The boy picked at the fur on the cuff of Pappy's sleeve.

"You can tell me, Charlie."

The boy continued picking at the fur. "I don't know who my daddy is."

"Uh-huh."

"You think you might see him?"

"It's possible. I'm supposed to know everybody in the world."

"Would you tell him something for me?"

Pappy leaned in close. "What's that?"

"I love him."

Had the boy glanced up, he would have seen tears on the rims of Pappy's eyes.

Pappy hugged the boy. "Charlie, I surely will. You got my word."

The boy put his arms around the neck of the man in the red suit and hugged him in return.

It was only when Pappy felt the boy's hug relax that he waved Junior over. "Would you take Charlie? I've got to talk to his mother."

"Sure, Pap—um, Santa." Junior lifted the boy into his arms. Charlie clung to him as the enormously tall elf moved away.

Pappy went to the mother. "It's Missus Jackson, isn't it? Can we talk some?"

He guided her to a chair at the side, away from the crowd. They sat together, Pappy and the boy's mother, her skin of ebony where Charlie's was a light chocolate. Pappy took her hands in his. "Missus Jackson, who's Charlie's dad?"

"Oh Lordy—" Grief and pain of times past welled up inside Nettie Jackson.

"It's important," Pappy said.

She brought a hand to her mouth, whispering, "Samuel—Samuel Phillips."

"Is he alive?"

"Think so. He calls me sometimes. Maybe once, twice a year."

"He in Knoxville?"

"Pretty sure."

"Do you know where?"

"No."

"What broke you two up?"

"Oh Lordy, Lordy, Lordy—" Nettie Jackson wept. She squeezed Pappy's hands hard, her fingernails sinking into his flesh as she fought for her composure. "Samuel, he was in Nam before I knew him, a soldier. War screwed him up something bad."

The tears and emotions, long repressed, rolled out. "I'd hold him at night, and he'd cry and shake for hours. Other times he'd run off and scream at the moon. When I got pregnant with Charlie, he was convinced the gooks was comin' for him. That's what he said. Gooks. He said he had to protect us by leavin'."

"Where'd he go?"

"Under the Gay Street bridge. Lived there with some other Nam crazies until the cops run them off. He come by a couple times after Charlie was born, to count little Charlie's fingers and toes, he said." Nettie Jackson took a handkerchief from inside the top of her dress. She wiped at her tears. "Samuel was in terrible shape."

"He wouldn't happen to have a nickname or anything others might know?"

"Pooch, yes. He said they called him Pooch because he could smell the Cong before anyone could hear 'em or see 'em."

"A point man."

"That's what he said."

"Missus Jackson, I'm an old soldier, way too old to have been in Vietnam. I was in another war, and like Charlie's dad, I saw more killing than anyone should in a lifetime." Pappy looked down at his boots, then back into the woman's eyes. "Look, I know where some of these boys hang out. I'm gonna try to find him."

"I wisht you wouldn't."

"Listen, I made your boy a promise." Pappy helped Nettie Jackson to her feet. He guided her across the room to Charlie laughing at Junior's ineptness with A Barrel of Monkeys, a game the boy had wanted.

"Charlie," Pappy said, "you take care of your momma. And you keep watch at the window. You and I, we may see each other one more time before Christmas."

The boy held up three monkeys he had hooked together, hand over tail. "You gonna come by?"

"Could be. I gotta go now." He touched a finger to the tip of Charlie's nose, then left him to search for Missus Claus—Doctor Ori-Anna Berry, advisor to the Theta Delta Theta sorority. He found her visiting with several of her Theta Delt helpers. "You up to a little adventure?"

"Always," she said as she excused herself from her girls.

"See that kid over there with Junior?"

"Yes."

"I'm gonna find his dad."

Without bothering to change to their civilian clothes, Pappy and Berry hurried out to Pappy's pickup in the University Center's parking ramp. He opened the door and helped Missus Claus in, then dashed around to the driver's side.

"Why you doing this?" Ori-Anna Berry asked after Pappy slid in behind the wheel.

"Every boy deserves to know his dad." He turned the ignition key, starting the engine, then backed the truck out of its parking slot. Pappy shifted the transmission into drive and aimed the truck down the ramp. "I lost my dad when I was ten, but at least I knew him and I can remember him. Charlie doesn't have that."

At the bottom of the exit ramp, he turned onto Stadium Drive, then Cumberland, heading west.

"Where are we going?" Berry asked.

"Fourth Creek. There's a jungle camp out there where the bums and the hobos stay. Most are Vietnam vets who can't stand the indoors."

"Strange."

"Not really. You're inside and something goes haywire, you've got only two ways to get out, the door and the window. To a foot soldier, that's not a good situation."

"And you know this how?"

"Doc, I was in the big Number Two—infantry, where war gets personal."

Lights flashed up in Pappy's windshield. They passed by.

Pappy hit his turn signal. He swung his pickup across twin on-coming lanes and onto a side street. From there, he cut right and left through a series of lesser streets, working his way west and south. After what seemed an eternity to Berry, but was perhaps only ten minutes, Pappy came out on a gravel trail that ended at a patch of winter-dried weeds.

Pappy stopped there. He killed the truck's motor and lights and sat silently listening to the distant whoop of an ambulance's siren fading as it traveled north toward Fort Sanders Hospital.

"Are we here?" Berry asked.

"We're close." Pappy opened the glove box. He took out a pint bottle of Jack Daniels and stuffed it inside his Santa jacket. He next reached under the seat for a black, long-barreled Magnum flashlight. He held it up for Berry to see. "A good light and a helluva weapon."

He slipped out his door, holding the button in as he closed it so the latch would not click.

Berry opened her door, and she, too, slipped out.

The two met in front of the truck. From there, they pushed out into a tangle of sumac and dried thistles that did their best to mask a little-used path, a path that after some time twisted down the side of a ravine. Twigs and branches snatched at the clothes of the intruders.

At the bottom, a creek—Fourth Creek—rippled over pebbles and stones as it made its way toward the Tennessee River. Here Pappy turned south, the direction in which the creek flowed, Berry two steps behind him.

Except for the sound of the occasional burble of water where the creek swelled up and rippled over a rock, all was silent.

Eerily silent.

No children playing late in backyards

No night birds.

Not even the city's sounds penetrated the ravine.

Pappy moved as silently as the night, Berry trying her best to be as quiet.

Thirty yards on, he put out his hand.

She stopped.

He flicked his flashlight on and aimed its beam down, inches ahead of the toe of his boot. The beam picked up a pale line not much thicker than a spider's silk.

Pappy knelt.

He touched it.

"Trip wire," he whispered. "Probably attached to some cans off in the brush. Cops come along, hit the line, the cans clatter and the bums scatter."

Pappy swept his gaze from one side of the path to the other as he eased back up. He stepped over the line and took Berry's hand, helped her across, then switched off the light.

Twenty paces on, the flames of a campfire created dancing shadows in the near distance. The muted voices of men drifted toward Pappy and Berry.

They went on toward the voices, easing up to the edge of a camp that was nothing more than a collection of cardboard shacks. Four men sat on milk crates around a fire.

Pappy stepped into the light. "Hello, boys."

Three looked up from their cigarettes and their bean cans of coffee.

"Good gawd, Sherm," said one, aiming his cigarette at Pappy, "is that a commie there in that red suit or is that old Sandy Claus?"

One of the others got to his feet, a mountain of a man. He stepped in front of Pappy. "Who the hell are you?"

"As your buddy says, Santa Claus."

"And I suppose that gawddamn slut in red is Missus Claus?" The man motioned to Berry.

"No slut, but you're right. She is Missus Claus."

"Smart ass."

Pappy stretched up. He pushed his face into the face of the taller man. "You lookin' to have me scratch your name off the good-little-boys' list?"

"No."

Pappy settled back on his heels. He scanned the man's faded and patched camouflage jacket. "You Army?"

"Hell no. Marine."

"Vietnam?"

"The DMZ."

"When?"

"What's it to you?"

"It's important."

"Sixty-Eight."

Pappy pulled his beard off. He stuffed it in his pocket. "Army, 'Forty-Two to 'Forty Five, all the hell over Europe."

"So we measured each other's dick." The ex-Marine punched a finger into Pappy's chest. "What the hell you want?"

"Samuel Phillips. Maybe you know him as Pooch."

"Never heard of him."

Pappy eased around the big man. He moved closer to the fire. "How about you boys? Any of you know Pooch?" Pappy, as he looked from one disheveled man to the next, pulled the pint of Jack Daniels from inside his jacket. He held it up. "A reward for the fella who helps me find him."

Two glanced at one another and shrugged. The third man raised a hand.

Pappy hunkered down, cradling the bottle. "Son, where is he?"

"I da-don't know. I ain't sa-sa-seen Pa-Pooch for th-th-three months."

"Guess you don't get this fine whiskey then."
Pappy straightened up.

The vet, in patched jeans and a Goodwill
mackinaw, rose up with him. "Ba-but Stick pra-
probably knows."

"Who's Stick?"

"He's one of our ba-boys, but he's ca-ca-crazy, all
those ch-chemicals in Nam and the wa-wack weed
he smokes."

"Where can I find him?"

The vet pointed downstream. "Fa-for that bottle,
I'll ta-take you to him."

"Think I can get along without you."

"He na knifes strangers."

An eyebrow raised. "Tell you what," Pappy said,
"you can split the bottle with Stick if you take me to
him *and* if he knows where Pooch is. Deal?"

The vet rubbed his hands on the sides of his coat,
his gaze fixed on the bottle. "Da-deal."

"What's your name, son?"

"Ca-Cooter . . . Wa-William Davis, my real na-
name."

"Call me Pappy."

"All right, Pa-Pappy." Davis started down the
path that led south out of the jungle camp, but
turned back. "Yer not ga-gonna renege now, are ya?"

"No sir. You got point. I'll watch your six."

"All right, I ga-got point." Davis turned and again
moved down the path. Pappy reached back for Ori-
Anna Berry's hand, and the two followed.

Minutes passed. The waning moon overhead
slipped behind low, scuddy clouds filled with snow.

Davis stopped. He cupped his hands around his mouth and let out a bobwhite whistle.

Silence.

Davis gave out with another bird call.

A bobwhite whistle echoed back.

"Stick?" Davis called out. "It's me, Ca-Cooter."

A scratchy throated "You alone?" came back.

"Na-not exactly."

"What do you mean, 'Na-not exactly?'"

"I got Sa-Sa-Sa-Santa Claus wa-with me."

Pappy glanced around for the voice.

"You jiggin' me, Coot? I'm a crazy sonuvabitch. Don't you jig me."

"I wa-wouldn't jig you, Stick. I ra-really do have a ga-guy here in a red suit."

"I'll kill him if he isn't Santa Claus."

Berry gripped Pappy's arm.

"He ra-really is, Stick," Cooter said to the night. "Ca-can we come in?"

Silence, except for the rhythmic scraping of steel on stone, someone whetting a knife.

"Yeah," the voice came back.

Davis turned to Pappy. "If you ga-got a beard, mister, you ba-better put it on."

Pappy took the beard from his pocket. Berry helped him hook the loops over his ears.

The trio moved on. Seconds ticked off into a half a minute, then a minute.

"That's far enough." The scratchy voice now came from behind the trio. Pappy turned. As he did, a light flashed in his face.

"Sonuvabitch," the voice croaked. "You makin' house calls in the bush, old man?"

"Appears so." Pappy flicked his Magnum on. Its beam shot down the other's and burst into a face that was more hair than skin. A hand came up to shield its eyes.

"Goddamn, that's bright."

"Yours ain't no sick candle either," Pappy said.

Stick lowered his flashlight.

Pappy did the same.

"What you want?" Stick asked.

"I'm looking for a friend of yours, Pooch Phillips."

"Why?"

"He's got a little boy he's not seen since the boy was a baby."

"What's his name?"

"This a test?" Pappy asked.

"Yeah."

"Charlie. Charlie Jackson."

"That's right."

"Damn right it's right."

"What do you want with Pooch?"

"The boy, for Christmas, he'd like to see his dad."

Stick waved his light for Pappy and the others to follow. He led them off the trail to a corrugated metal shack under a rock overhang, a shack masked from the outside world by a thick tangle of sumac with a honey locust tree standing sentinel.

The vet struck a match. He put the flame to a candle in a snuff can. "Pooch ain't here as you can see."

"Where is he?"

Stick, in railroad overalls, denim jacket and fatigue cap, flopped in a canvas camp chair. The muzzle of Kalashnikov poked from beneath a blanket on the ground, the weapon close to the vet's hand. "VA hospital. I carried him in sometime back."

"What's wrong?"

"He's dying."

Pappy hunkered down. He brought the Jack Daniels bottle out and set it next to the candle. "What of?"

"Nam." Stick spit to the side. "Nam's killed all my friends."

Cooter piped up. "It ain't ka-killed me."

"It will, Coot. It's gonna kill you and me both. We just don't know when." Stick saw Pappy staring at the books on the rock wall behind him. "Like 'em?" he asked.

"Yeah. What's that big one, *Plato's Republic?*"

"Uh-huh." Stick reached back for the book. He tossed it to Pappy.

Pappy caught it. He ran his hand over the cover before he opened it. "Leather, nice. You read this?"

"Sure."

"It's in Greek."

"Uh-huh. And I got books in I-talian, French, German, and Russian. I read 'em all. I may be bugs, man, but I ain't stupid." Stick gazed out over the bushes that shielded him from the world beyond, his eyes taking in the first flakes of snow drifting down from the scud clouds. "Might be a white Christmas."

Stick closed his eyes.

Pappy waited for the scholar of the jungle camp to leave the world inside his being, to again open his eyes. When he did, Pappy placed the Plato book in Stick's hands. "Pooch . . . When did you see him last?"

The Vietnam vet held the book tenderly, as one would a baby. "Couple days ago."

"How's he doing?"

"Weak, coughing up his guts. Pooch was in the back country, like a lot of us when they were spraying that Agent Orange. Soaked him and his platoon time and again."

"I've been told it's bad," Pappy said.

"Blisters, headaches that go on forever, pain, deformed children. Gawddamn right it's bad. Pooch is the last of his platoon he knows of. All the others—" Stick's hand flicked out flat.

Pappy tapped the vet's knee. "I'm gonna see him. You want to come along?"

"You got room in your sleigh for a mean old fart like me?"

"Always," Pappy said as he stood up.

Stick looked from the red-suited man to the bottle in its black label. "That for me?"

"For you and Cooter."

"Think I'll stay here. Coot an' me, we'll kill that old sucker." Stick picked up the bottle. He held it aloft in a salute to Pappy. "Merry Christmas."

"WHERE do you suppose he came up with those leather-bound books?" Ori-Anna Berry asked from the dark comfort of her side of the cab, the windshield wipers swishing, beating a metronome's beat as they brushed away snowflakes that wanted to cling to the glass.

Pappy leaned forward, his forearms on the steering wheel. He glanced to the right, past Berry, looking for approaching traffic as he came on an intersection. None, so Pappy rolled on through. "We all collect something."

He popped the cigarette lighter. Pappy pulled a Camel from the open pack on his dashboard and put the tip between his lips. When the lighter snapped out, he touched it to the end of his cigarette. "Mind if I smoke?"

"Yes."

Pappy's hand stopped in mid-air. "I shoulda asked before I fired up, shouldn't I?"

He slid the lighter back in its socket, then traded hands on the wheel so he could roll his window down. Pappy flicked the cigarette out into the night air, the glowing end spinning away.

"VA Hospital coming up," Berry said.

Pappy slowed. He turned the steering wheel to the left and guided his truck into a traffic circle that swung past the central building on the VA campus. He drove on to a World War Two barracks building and there wheeled into a parking space that had a 'Reserved for Doctor' sign attached to a post in front of it.

"Mister Brown, you can't park here."

"You're a doc."

"Not that kind."

"Who's gonna know?" Pappy shut off the lights and cut the motor. He opened his door. "Come on, Missus Claus, let's go hunting."

Berry sighed.

She opened her door and stepped out and down into a skiff of snow. "Is the door going to be open?" she asked when the two met on the sidewalk.

"There's always the night buzzer."

Pappy knew the place well, not from being a patient, but from being a visitor to the survivors of his war.

He knew well, too, the cemetery at the rear of the campus, the destination for the old men who lived out their last years here, those who had no families to carry them home when they died. Pappy served in the rifle squad that fired the last volley at their funerals.

The reception desk was vacant when the two came in out of the weather. Pappy looked first down the main hallway, then the side, both dimly lit and as vacant of people as the lobby.

He leaned on the desk, drumming his fingers.

"Oh, the hell with it," Pappy muttered and marched around to the nurses' side. There he opened the master book and ran a finger down the pages of patients. "Here he is. Room Twenty-six. And he's got a bunk mate, Cyril Roberts. My gawd, I know old Cyril."

Pappy came around the desk. He took Berry's hand and the two set off, Pappy checking the numbers at the side of each door. Televisions glowed from several of the rooms, the sound turned low.

They stopped when they came to Twenty-six. There Pappy tapped on the door frame.

A bedside light snapped on.

"Yeah?" a voice asked.

Pappy leaned in. "Cyril?"

A big-framed old man pushed himself up on his elbow. He was rail thin, a craggy nose prominent on his face, slightly offset, a nose that looked more like a beak, and beneath it a handlebar mustache as white as Pappy's beard. "Good golly, is that you, Sandy Claus?"

Pappy pulled his beard down as he came in. "Pappy Brown. You remember me?" He sat on the bed.

Roberts' visage brightened. He hugged Pappy and slapped him on the back with his oversized boney hands, the fingers bent to the side by arthritis. "Willie Joe, how could I forget you? When the county condemned my shit house, you built me an indoor toilet and a septic tank, and you wouldn't take a dime."

"Hell, Cyril, you didn't have any dimes. You were on an Army pension."

Roberts leaned back. He clamped Pappy's shoulders in his hands and looked deep into his eyes. "I ain't dead yet, Old Scout. I hope you ain't come up here to be in my funeral."

"I hope I'm not in your funeral until you reach a hundred."

"Eleven years, Willie boy. Eleven years and I'll be a century man." Roberts looked over Pappy's shoulder. "Who's that behind you? Missus Claus?"

"A friend," Pappy said.

"Well, what brings you by?"

Pappy glanced to the side, to an empty bed, the blanket smooth, the pillow undisturbed, precisely placed an equal distance from either side of the bed. "You've got a roommate?"

"Pooch?"

"We've come to see him. Where is he?"

"Out back, smoking." Roberts beckoned for Pappy to lean in. "Between you an' me, Pooch shouldn't be smokin'. Got this gawd-awful cough."

As if it were a cue, they heard coughing in the hallway, a harsh, hacking cough repeating, moving toward Room Twenty-six. It stopped and a man, more emaciated than Roberts, wheezing, entered, his gaze fixed on the floor before him, the man in faded jeans, a khaki shirt and slippers, his shoulders hunched, a hand holding a handkerchief to his mouth.

"Pooch, you got company."

Pooch Phillips looked up, startled. When he saw strangers in his room, he stepped back into the doorway.

"Pooch, it's all right." Roberts rested hand on Pappy's shoulder. "These is good people."

"Maybe so, Sarge," Phillips said. "I'll talk from here. Who you, mister?"

Pappy did not move from where he sat on the edge of Roberts' bed. "Pappy Brown," he said. "You got a little boy?"

"Yeah. Something happen to him?"

"He's all right. When did you see him last?"

"Six years ago."

Roberts squared his shoulders. The softness in his eyes disappeared, replaced by fierce anger. "You got a boy, an' you ain't seen him fer six years? What in the name of good gravy is wrong with you?"

Phillips raised a hand. "Sarge, it's hard to explain."

"By gawd, it's time you did. If I had a boy, I'd be outta here faster'n—"

"Look at me, Sarge," Phillips said. "I'm in a helluva shape. I don't want no son of mine seeing me like this."

"Stick says you're dying," Pappy said, not moving from his seat on the bed. "That true?"

"You know Stick?"

Pappy nodded.

"Ain't we all? Some just sooner than others." Phillips, tiring, leaned against the jamb.

"Charlie wants to see you."

Phillips' gaze went down to the floor, then to the dull steel sink in the corner of the room. "How would you know, mister?"

"I'm Santa Claus. I know everything."

"No, really, how would you know?"

"Look at me, son," Pappy said. "I'm a student at the university, an oooold student. You may find that hard to believe, but believe it. I've got a roommate, and he's Charlie's Big Brother—you know, the Big Brother, Big Sister program?"

Pooch smiled—not genuine—his eyes a bit vacant.

"Charlie having a Big Brother," Pappy went on, "it's not the same as having a father. He's got one wish for Christmas, for me to tell you he loves you, but you owe it to this little boy you created to go see him."

"I can't."

"You want Charlie's only memory of you to be of you laid out in a box?"

"I didn't know my father," Phillips said.

"So you want that for your son?"

"No."

Roberts waved for Phillips to come to his bed. "Pooch, look, you get your bee-hind in gear and you go see that boy. I don't know if yer a believin' man, but I am, and I can tell you you're not long from having to explain to God a whole lotta things, and you want to explain this one right."

"I can't do it, Sarge."

"You want to live out the rest of your days with me, son?"

"'Course I do."

"Then git. Willie Joe, where's this boy live?"

"Couple miles from here."

Roberts, his hand unsteady, gestured at a locker on the far side of the room. "Pooch, ya put yer coat on. This man an' this woman, they'll take you by right now."

"Maybe tomorrow."

"Pooch—son—none of us knows we got tomorrow."

Phillips looked into Roberts' watery eyes, softening, about to spill over. He started to open his mouth, but Roberts raised a bent finger in warning.

Unable to run and no longer able to hide, Phillips gave it up. Dumbly, he went to the locker and rattled the door open.

Pappy handed his ignition keys to Berry. "Take him out to my truck. I gotta make a call."

Phillips glanced back. "You ain't got a sleigh?"

"A Dodge Ram. I'm a modern Santa."

BERRY had the pickup running and the heater blasting out hot air by the time Pappy caught up. She sat behind the wheel while Phillips paced in the snow. Berry rolled the window down. "He won't get in," she said to Pappy.

"Nuts."

He went over to Phillips. Pappy attempted to put an arm around the man's shoulders, to ask what the difficulty was, but Phillips pulled away. Pappy, angered, squared around in front of him. "What the hell is your problem?"

Phillips shook like a blanket in the wind. "I can't ride in that cab. It's too close in there."

"Well, you sure can't ride in the box. You'll freeze yer britches off."

"I can't sit in the center of that seat!"

Pappy ran his tongue along his teeth, the lower first, then the upper, sucking at them. "Tell you what, what if I were to sit in the center and you take shotgun? You get to feeling closed in, you roll the window down. How's that?"

"We can try it."

Pappy shot a hand in the air. He spun around, opened the passenger door, and hopped in. "You're driving," he said to Berry as he slid over beside her.

Phillips followed Pappy, somewhat tentatively, his gaze roaming the interior of the cab as he eased his rear down on the seat.

"Gawd, Pooch, close the door before all the heat gets out."

Phillips pulled the door into its frame, shifting about when he heard the latch click.

"It's all right, boy." Pappy put his hand on Phillips' knee, to assure him, but Phillips pushed the hand away.

Berry moved the shift lever from park to reverse. "How do I get where we're going?"

"Go downtown, then hook north on Gay."

Berry backed out of the parking slot. The truck slid when she stepped on the brake pedal. "Lordy, it's slick."

"The city streets will be better."

Berry pulled the shift lever into drive. She pressed down lightly on the gas, and the truck crept away.

Phillips' wandering gaze came to rest on the cigarette pack on the dash. "Can I have one?"

Pappy put his hand over the pack. "Sorry, the doc here—Missus Claus—she don't allow any smoking in here. Now if you and me were alone—"

Berry shot a look at Pappy meant to pierce armor as she herded the truck onto the street.

Phillips jerked his jaw to the side. "Nettie still live in that little house of hers?"

"On New Street?"

"Yeah."

"She does."

Phillips looked out the side window. "First couple years, most nights I watched that house from across the street."

"Nobody complain about you hanging around?"

"Nobody saw me. I was invisible, man. In Nam, if they could see you, you were dead. I got real good at being invisible."

A rotating yellow light came up in the windshield. It passed by, attached to a city truck, its blade down, slush curling off to the side, splattering parked cars.

"Why'd you watch the place, Pooch?" Pappy asked.

Phillips shrugged. "I s'pose I thought I was protecting what was mine."

"But why not just go in?"

"I couldn't bring myself to do it." A tremor ran through Phillips' shoulders. He cracked the window, then rolled it down halfway. "Closed places. Can't stand closed places."

"But you stay at the hospital."

"That's different."

"How so?" Pappy asked.

"They let me come and go. If they said, 'Pooch, you gotta stay in that damn room,' I'd be jumpin' out the window. I'd be gone, man. . . . Nettie, she still pretty as I remember?"

"Gay ahead," Berry said.

"Go left. At Summit Hill, it's a right."

Berry pulled the turn signal lever down.

Pappy glanced at Phillips. "Pretty? Let me put it this way. She's had a hard life, trying to raise those four little children by herself. That takes a toll on a body, Pooch. But I think if you were to ask your boy, Charlie would tell you his momma's the prettiest woman in the whole world. There's a lotta love between those two."

Phillips grew silent. He turned within himself, absently gazing out the passenger window.

Berry stopped at the red light at Summit Hill Drive, then turned right.

Summit Hill curved down through an old warehouse district that had not known prosperity for thirty years. Then it climbed away east, up over the James White Parkway to Summit Hill proper.

Pappy waggled a finger. "Left on Old Vine."

Berry slowed. She pulled the turn-signal handle down.

"Old Vine's going to curve a couple times. Beyond the second curve, it's left on New Street. New Street, that's a joke. There's nothing new about it."

South of Summit Hill Drive, high on the hill, were apartment complexes, the residents largely white and largely young.

North of the Drive, on the land that fell away toward First Creek, were the projects, the residents largely black, all ages and hordes of children.

New, for its short length, paralleled First Creek.

The headlights flashed on a street sign. "There it is," Berry said.

"Left. Third house on the left, next to the alley."

Berry pulled the turn signal lever down. It set to clicking. She took her foot from the gas pedal to the brake, turning the steering wheel as she did.

"No! NO!!" Phillips threw open the passenger door and bolted from the rolling truck.

Pappy lunged for him but missed. He leaped out and hot-footed it after the vet racing away, up the sidewalk.

Phillips slid in the snow. He made the turn into the alley and pounded off, Pappy less than a dozen paces behind but fading, his arms milling at the air as he ran. *What the hell am I doing this for?*

Pappy saw a silver trash can ahead. He grabbed the lid as he passed and whirled, flinging the lid as hard as he could at Phillips' fleeing figure.

The giant frisbee sailed out flat. It clipped Phillips behind the knees, knocking him off stride. He stumbled, then fell, sprawling, sliding face first in the snow, a coughing fit racking his body.

Pappy trotted up, his chest heaving. Before Pooch could rise, Pappy stepped on him. "You sonuvabitch! I'm too gawddamn old for this. You tryin' to give me a heart attack?"

He grabbed Phillips by the collar. Pappy hauled him up, Phillips still coughing, and shagged him back up the alley.

"Lost my slippers," Phillips wheezed.

"Serves you right, knothead."

"I ain't no knothead."

"Coward then. You prefer coward?"

Phillips raised his arm to his face. He coughed horribly against his sleeve, doubling over.

Pappy moved aside.

"I prefer not bein' here," Phillips said between gasps for air.

"The hell with what you prefer. You're here so your boy can see his dad, to know he's got one. You want to argue about that, I'll beat hell out of you."

"I can't go in there without shoes."

"Charlie's not gonna notice. Come on." Pappy hauled him along.

"I don't know what to say."

"It'll come."

"You gonna wait on me?"

"Knothead. The way you ran on me? And that damn Stick said you were weak."

"You gonna wait?"

Pappy and Phillips shambled through the beams from the headlights of Pappy's truck, Pappy not loosening his grip on the man's collar. "Yeah, I'm gonna wait."

He pushed Phillips up the steps to the porch of a one-story bungalow, its paint peeling, a bare yellow bug light on above the door.

Pappy banged on the side of the house.

Seconds passed before the door creaked open. Nettie Jackson, in a terry-cloth robe and flip-flops, stood before the late-night callers.

"Missus Jackson," Pappy said, his chest still heaving as he worked to catch his breath, "I brought Charlie an early Christmas present. His pap."

He slapped Phillips on the back of the head. "Take your cap off."

Phillips raked his cap from his head. "Nettie?"

Nettie Jackson stepped back. "You better come in, Samuel, a-fore you catch your death of cold. Charlie's in the bed, but I'll get him up."

Barefooted, Pooch Phillips shuffled in. He turned back to stare at Pappy hanging onto the door jamb.

Nettie peered around Phillips. "Comin' in, Mister Brown?"

"No, I'll be in the way. My truck's across the street. I'll wait there."

"You look like you been runnin' some."

"Some, yeah."

"You know you're welcome."

"Nettie, I know. That's all right."

Pappy stepped back and Nettie Jackson closed the door, but not before he saw the aluminum Christmas tree in the corner and the presents in their opened wrappings under it, the presents from the Tau Upsilon/Theta Delta Theta party.

Pappy grimaced as he turned to leave. He grabbed for the calf of his right leg.

Berry saw him crumple and came running from the truck. "What is it!"

"Charlie horse." Pappy massaged the muscle. "Gawddamn it hurts."

Berry got an arm under his shoulder. She helped Pappy limp down the steps and across the street, but he stopped her when she reached for the truck door.

"Eeeyeah! Oh my leg. Just let me down on the running board."

She helped him turn and sit, then sat beside him as he kneaded at the pain in his calf muscle. "Hard work being Santa Claus, isn't it?"

Pappy flinched. "No wonder he's old."

Note: This is not the first of my Cody & Me stories, but it is the best. Cody Debbs and Derek Wilson are two middle-school-aged guys. Derek tells most of the stories in essays he writes for his teacher.

Derek Wilson
Mrs. Engstrom's class
Marshall Middle School
January 5

Christmas at my house

I don't know about you, Mrs. Engstrom, but my mom starts decorating for Christmas late, like the week before. Like on Monday before Christmas, she has my dad get out the stepladder and put up garland all around the living room. Then he brings down her collection of nutcrackers from the attic, and the best go on the mantel with the ballet shoes Mom wore when she danced in the Nutcracker Ballet when she was my age. My mom was once a kid, can you believe that? I don't.

Anyway, then comes the Christmas tree. It's always almost twice as tall as my dad because we have high ceilings in our old house. Anyway, we don't decorate our tree until Christmas Eve. It's a tradition, Mom says.

This year, my Uncle Bill from Florida brought his family up, to beat Santa Claus here he said. His family includes my cousin Normie. Normie's four and a real pain in the butt. I didn't mean to write that, Mrs. Engstrom, but he is.

After Christmas Eve dinner, which is always brats and sauerkraut—it's a tradition, Mom says—we get the Christmas tree all decorated, well, almost. Dad's up on the stepladder, finishing, leaning way out to put the star on the top of the tree, and Uncle Bill's holding the ladder, keeping it steady, when Normie decides to pull my dog Rex's tail. Rex, he doesn't like that, so he whips around just as Mom was bringing in hot chocolate for everybody. And Rex bangs into Mom, and the cups of hot chocolate go off the tray onto Uncle Bill who leaps back, and the ladder and my dad go over into the tree, and the tree goes down with a crash, and the star catches on the garland and all the garland comes down.

Mom, she sees the garland pulling away from the mantel, and she runs to stop it, but it's too late. The garland rakes off her nutcracker collection and Great Grandma's antique oil lamp with it that we've got up on the mantel. The lamp's lighted because we always and only light it on Christmas Eve—it's a tradition, my Mom says—and it breaks and sets the tree on fire.

Uncle Bill sees that. He pulls Dad out, and they run to the kitchen for our fire extinguisher, but it only dribbles out a little powder. Dad's yelling for Uncle Bill to get the water hose up from the basement and for me to call 911, and I do while he's flailing at the flames with his sweater. But before anyone answers, three firemen bust through our front door with fire extinguishers of their own and put out the fire. They were going back to the station from an accident call, they tell us, when they saw the fire through our window.

Mom was so happy the house didn't burn down that she made hot chocolate again, for everybody this time and insisted the firemen stay and have dessert with us, and Dad pours a round of Leinenkugel Stout and brings out cigars that he insists the firemen smoke with him and Uncle Bill, the cigar making Uncle Bill sick, and he up-chucks on Normie. Well, Normie deserved it, the pain in the butt.

Anyway, Mrs. Engstrom, Mom says this will be the Christmas she won't ever forget, and neither will I, I guess. Poor Rex, his tail's bent now, so I don't think he'll forget it either.

Note: I wrote this story as a part of my first AJ Garrison crime novel, *The Watch*. My writers group made me cut it. They said, and rightly so, it has nothing to do with the mystery. But it's a neat Christmas story. It's 1967. We're in eastern Tennessee, in the foothills of the Great Smokies. Enjoy.

Holly & Mistletoe

WILL CLICK, a hard-muscled retired Air Force pilot, rested himself against the side of a U-Haul trailer while Scotty Moore, the poster image of a state police trooper, fumbled with the key for the padlock. Moore wore his Saturday casual, a sweatshirt emblazoned with a shoe print and the words 'Knoxville Flatfeet.'

"You know," Click said, "this is a gawd awful time to be moving, two days before Christmas."

"Divorce came through. No reason to stay up in Knoxville any longer."

"Yeah, and my girl didn't have anything to do with this."

Moore grinned at the mention. "Oh, I wouldn't say that didn't have something to do with deciding to move here rather than, say, Strawberry Plains."

He twisted the key in the lock. After the mechanism released, Moore put the padlock in his pocket and swung the trailer's double doors open.

Click came around. He peered inside. "That's it? That's all you got?"

"That's all the divorce left me."

"My gawd, looks like the junk dorm students put on the curb when spring semester's over."

Moore hauled out a Jack Daniels box filled with books. He hefted it to Click. "This is my dorm stuff."

"You never threw any of it away?"

"No chance. It went straight from the dorm to Barb's and my first apartment. Combined with her stuff, we called it old college, early matrimony."

"Jeez."

A head poked out from an upstairs window of a rambling two-story that had known sweeter times. "Scott?"

Moore swung around. He peered up at the smudged face of AJ Garrison—Will Click's lawyer daughter—the sleeves of her University of Tennessee sweatshirt bunched above her elbows. "Yeah?"

"Have you got any bleach?"

"No. Why?"

"You've got rust stains and mineral deposits in the bathroom sink and the toilet. The Comet won't take them out."

"Muriatic acid," Click whispered.

"How's that?"

"Muriatic acid. That's what you need. I got a jug at the house."

Moore hollered up to Garrison. "Your dad says muriatic acid! He's got some."

"You ready to bring your things in?"

"Yeah!"

"Well, put everything on the landing. I don't want you and Pop tracking up your clean floors."

Moore glanced at Click whose only response was a shrug.

"Right," Moore called out.

Garrison pulled back inside, and the window slid closed.

"Well, let's do it," Click said.

The 'everything' turned out to be eight liquor boxes of books, a pile of boards and bricks for a bookcase, a card table accompanied by four folding chairs, only two of which matched the table, a couch that sagged like a bear had slept on it for an overly long winter, a plastic chair in the shape of a hand, a glass-topped coffee table, a Bush's Beans box labeled 'kitchen stuff,' a Corn Flakes case labeled 'bedroom stuff,' a Sugar Pops case labeled 'stuff stuff,' two suitcases, a gym bag, a rollaway bed, and a black-and-white TV with a coat hanger for an antenna. Moore and Click schlepped it all inside and up the stairs to where they stacked it on the second-floor landing. Did it all in under forty-five minutes.

Moore opened the door to the flat only to hear Garrison's voice coming his way from back in the kitchen, "Take your shoes off before you come in here."

"She always so bossy?"

"Ever since she was a little kid. Mind of her own, always had to be in charge."

Moore settled on the top step. He unlaced his hiking boots. Click, on the arm of the couch, pulled off a shoe. He massaged his ankle.

"This is embarrassing," Moore said.

"What's that?"

He held up his foot. Two toes aired themselves through a hole in the end of his sock.

Click took off his other shoe. A toe poked its way into the light from the end of his sock. Click wiggled his toe, showing it off. "No wife to mend for me either."

Garrison bustled out onto the landing. She stared at her father and his holey sock, then gave a look of disdain to Moore's bare toes. "You two are the cheapest. I think you both could part with a dollar and a half for new socks."

Click admired his wiggling toe. "I'm on a pension."

"Took all my money," Moore said, "just to set up housekeeping here."

"Gawd." Garrison picked up the 'kitchen stuff' carton and huffed inside with it.

After a moment, Moore slapped Click's leg. "Well, let me give you the cook's tour."

The two rose and shuffled on into the flat in their stockinged feet, the first room smelling of Pine-sol and Pledge. Click's eyes widened. "My golly, Miss Molly, you could hold a square dance in here."

"Big, isn't it? I'm thinking of putting my grand pianah over there in front of the bay winder." Moore snickered.

"You're going to put your Christmas tree there," Garrison said from the kitchen.

"I don't have a Christmas tree!"

"Well, get one."

This time it was Moore who shrugged.

Click cocked his head to one side. His gaze fell on a fireplace that had rose tiling on the hearth and up the sides to a carved cherry mantelpiece. "That work, the fireplace?"

"You know, I never asked."

The oak floor gleamed with new wax Garrison had put down.

"Nice," Click said. "You have to do much work on the place?"

"AJ didn't tell you?"

"No, I've been away a lot. Charter flying."

"Then you missed it all."

"I guess."

Moore patted a wall painted cream. "There was wallpaper here and in all the rooms—tired stuff, dirty up to waist high from the hands of little kids. I didn't mind it much, but AJ said I had to rent a steamer."

"Stripped the walls, huh?"

"Then we had to spackle the cracks in the plaster—lotta cracks—and we painted. But there was a benefit to it all."

"Yeah?"

"Missus Caudileski, my landlady, she liked what we did and knocked off half a month's rent."

Garrison's voice came from the kitchen. "Tell Pop about the light fixture."

Moore went to the middle of the room. He stood beneath a brass chandelier. "The light that was here, AJ thought it was too small, so Missus C goes rummaging in the basement, and she finds this chandelier. The three of us spent one evening polishing the brasswork and washing the globes. Then I wired it up, even put a dimmer on it."

Click admired the finished product. He chuckled about something he saw and, without saying anything, followed Moore back to the kitchen where they came on Garrison and Mabel Caudileski unpacking the 'kitchen stuff.'

"Missus C," Moore said, "I didn't know you were here."

She held up two State Police mugs. "This all you have for coffee?"

"Missus C, I'm a bachelor now."

"What are you going to do when you have company?"

"I guess I'll break out the straws."

"You're hopeless, young man, you know that?"

"Hopelessly in love with you."

"Don't I wish." She looked beyond Moore to Click. "I'm so glad to have this young man living above me. I didn't know who I'd find for a renter in the dead of winter, and him a policeman."

"A trooper," Garrison said. She picked three Melmac plates and a cereal bowl out of the 'stuff' box and placed them on a shelf.

"That is what I said, a policeman. Mister Moore—"

"I'd rather you call me Scotty."

Missus C touched a mug to the front of his sweatshirt. "Mister Scotty, I have to ask. What's Knoxville Flatfeet?"

"That was our baseball team—all Knoxville cops."

The eyebrows of the big-boned woman knitted together.

"Flat feet, get it?" Moore asked.

"Sorry, I don't."

"That's all right. All you need to know is we were good. We went twenty-eight and two in the summer league."

"It's a man thing," Garrison said to Missus C, the older woman in a misshapen house dress and lace-up shoes that came up over her ankles. "Scotty, show Pop your bedroom."

"All right. Will, we might as well set up the bed while we're at it."

He and Click went back to the front room, Moore hauling off his sweatshirt on the way. He shook it out and hung it and his cap on a coat tree that had curled arms. "Missus C loaned me this until I can get something of my own," he said of the tree. Moore ran his fingers back through his hair, strands of gray showing at the temples.

Click slipped out of his leather flight jacket. He hung it on one of the arms, but he kept his knit cap on.

On the landing, they picked up the bed—folded up and secure—and carried it on inside. In silent communication, they lifted it high so the wheels wouldn't mar the waxed floor. Moore guided to his right, into a short hallway, then through a door into a second, but smaller, front room—the bedroom.

He and Click positioned the bed before they unlatched the ends and let the frame and mattress fold out. Click sat on the bed—tested it—the springs making stretchy music beneath his bottom. "Not exactly quiet, is it?"

"It didn't keep me awake at college, though my roommate complained a lot."

Click peered underneath. "How about you hook your radio antenna wire to the springs? I betcha you could get WSM out of Nashville—the Grand Ol' Opry."

"You listen to that?"

"Sometimes. AJ thinks it's corn. But then I think some of the music she listens to is kinda strange. The Byrds—don't understand 'em—and Janis Joplin, all she does is scream."

Moore went to the side window. "Come look at this."

Click got up, the bed's springs sproinging back. He joined Moore at the window. "East window, you're going to get the morning sun."

"Nice way to wake up, huh?"

Click gazed out beyond the house and its side yard. "Hey, you can see up into the mountains from here."

"Well, Cullowhee at least." But Moore gestured toward a bare-branched tree much closer, just beyond the porch roof. "That's what I wanted you to see, that apple tree."

"Know what you got there?"

"Yes, an apple tree."

Click chuckled. "It's not just any apple tree. That's a Virginia Beauty. Fruit sweet like cherries."

"Really?"

"It's an old-timey apple. You're going to love the fruit from that tree."

"How do you know so much about it?"

"I used to help Mister Caudileski pick for part of the harvest. Virginia Beauties, good keepers. My wife wouldn't have anything else." Click rubbed the thick muscle between his neck and shoulder as memories came flowing up from the far reaches of his mind. "The old tree kind of got away after Mister C died. Maybe you should offer to prune it and spray it, bring it back into shape."

"Yes—well, what I wanted to tell you is what Missus C told me."

"Uh-huh?"

"This was her boys' room when they were kids."

"I can picture that."

"They'd sneak out at night—go out this window, cross the roof, and climb down that tree."

"Scotty, this is a great house for kids."

Moore jerked his jaw. He turned away to a door and opened it. He pulled a chain on a bare-bulb light fixture. "This is the only closet on the second floor. Big enough, huh?"

"For what little you've got."

Moore pulled the chain again, returning the closet to darkness. He led Click out and across the hall to the back bedroom. "I'm thinking of setting up my office here," he said, pointing to where things might go. "Put a door across a couple two-drawer files for a desk, I could write up my reports here, keep my law books over there. Did you know we get tested every six months on the statutes we're expected to enforce?"

"And I thought we commercial pilots had it tough."

"All of us troopers, we have a lot we have to read." Moore felt the padlock in his pocket. He pulled the lock out and went back to the closet where he parked the padlock and its key on a shelf.

"I go further than most," he said when he came back. "I read the court cases and the judges' opinions, particularly those from the state supreme court."

Click moved around this back bedroom-cum-office, springing on the balls of his feet, as if he were testing the soundness of the floor. He stopped in one corner and gazed at Moore. "You could put bunk beds in here, you know. Bring your kids down."

The trooper gave a quick shake of his head.

"Why not?"

"Barb wanted custody. I didn't contest it. A cop's life is hell on a marriage."

"I s'pose."

Moore didn't respond. After some moments of silence, he led the way back out into the hall.

"Bathroom down there," he said, waving a hand toward an open door.

Click drifted that way. He leaned in. "Would you look at that, an old claw-foot tub just like the one I've got."

"I'd prefer a shower, but the tub's it."

"In Nam, we'd tell each other stories on what we missed most about home. I said for me it was soaking in a tub. You get so hog dirty in a war." Click glanced back over his shoulder. "You in Nam?"

Moore pulled at the front of his T-shirt. "Germany. Army made me an MP and shipped me to Krautland."

"Nice duty?"

"When you weren't cracking heads in the bars on Saturday nights, yeah."

"Kids get away from home, they want to raise a little hell."

"I guess."

A voice interrupted. "Are you two old duffers going to bore each other, or are you going to bring in the couch?"

At the end of the hall stood Garrison, her hands braced against her hips.

Moore saluted. "Well, get to it."

"Yes ma'am. Right away, ma'am," Click said.

"Missus C and I've started lunch. You've got fifteen minutes."

"But I don't have any groceries."

"Scott, I know where the store is."

He raised his hands in surrender.

"Smart boy," Click whispered. "Never argue."

Again Garrison disappeared back into the kitchen.

Moore and Click went out onto the landing. They wrestled the shabby couch in through the doorway and set it against the long wall. Moore shimmed a leg with a magazine.

"Sad lookin' thing," Click said.

"It is, but I'll throw a blanket over it."

"Sure be an improvement."

Next they toted in the boards, three long ones—eight feet each—and two short ones.

They went back out for the bricks. Click studied the pile. "There is a way to get them inside faster than carrying them. You up for a game of catch?"

Moore rubbed his hands on his jeans. "I suppose you want to be the pitcher?"

"Well, it is my idea. Anyway, you know how many bricks you want in each stack before you put a board across. I don't."

Moore dashed inside. He slid up beside the boards and crouched for the first catch.

Click lofted a brick to him.

Moore snatched it from the air and slapped it in place on the floor.

Two more bricks came flying. Moore snagged both. He set them a short distance to either side of the first brick, then positioned the first long board across them.

Click fired in another brick and another. He kept pitching until Moore had his stacks tall enough that he could position the second board.

Click brightened. "How about we pick up the pace?" he said and let fly with a barrage of bricks, Moore grabbing them, stacking them, his forehead slicking up from sweat.

A brick sailed past Moore. It banged off the wall, gouging the plaster.

"What are you two doing out there?"

Moore froze, as did Click.

"Nothing," Moore said.

The word came as an automatic reflex, of a boy caught doing something he knew he shouldn't.

He and Click waited for the worst.

When Garrison didn't come out, Moore relaxed, and Click, too. Click mopped his face with his shirt sleeve, then set about gathering up the last of the bricks. Moore scrambled after the errant one halfway across the room.

With that brick and Click's, Moore built out the bookcase and topped the unit with the short boards to either side, creating a well in the middle. He lifted his television into that space. Moore plugged the TV in. He snapped the 'On' switch on, and static crackled through the cheap speaker in the television's plastic cabinet. The black on the picture tube gave way to snow.

"If I want to see snow, I just look out the window," Click said.

Moore twiddled with the coat hanger. The swirling flakes let up, and 'The Days of Our Lives' came through. "Ahh, my favorite soap."

"You kidding?"

"Of course." He snapped the television off.

"Do you have the table set up?" Garrison asked from the bowels of the kitchen.

"Not yet."

"Well, get to it. We're bringing out the dogs."

"The what?"

"You'll see."

Click skated back out to the landing. There he yanked a card table from the clutter that had come up from the trailer. He flung the table through the doorway. Moore grabbed the table out of the air. He snapped the legs out and set the table down in front of the bay window.

Click slid up beside Moore, two folding chairs in each hand. "You can really move on this floor, you know that?"

The two did a 'ta-da' and held their hands out to the table and chairs just so as Garrison came in from the kitchen. She gave Moore and her father an indulgent smile as one might give to idiot children.

She carried a platter of buns and hot dogs from which rose vaporous steam. Missus C followed with a serving tray laden with bowls of chili, coleslaw, onions, sweet pickle relish, and the other stuff of lunch, including a bag of taco chips she clutched in her fingers curled beneath the tray. "I've got a pan of mint brownies in the kitchen I baked for you for dessert."

"And ice cream," Garrison said as she dealt out the paper plates and napkins.

Missus C put her tray on the table, and Garrison waved for everyone to sit.

Click snatched off his cap. He stuffed it in his pocket before he pulled a chair out for Missus C. She sat down, and he took the chair to her right.

Garrison didn't wait for Moore to be a gentleman. She slipped into the chair to Missus C's left before he could reach for it.

Moore—the last standing—settled on the only vacant chair. It faced across the table to Missus C.

Click glanced at Garrison. He pointed a finger up, then down. She nodded and said to Moore, "Take my hand."

"Why?"

"We're going to pray."

"I don't do that."

"You do today."

Click bowed.

The others followed his lead.

"Gracious God," he said, his voice hushed, "we thank You for food, for warmth, for roofs over our heads, for good friends and good family. You have blessed us so richly. We know, of course, that the richest blessing is the birth of Your Son, placed here to bring us to You. Help us to remember that that is the reason for this time, for this season. We ask now Your blessing on these simple foods, that they may keep us strong so we can do the chores at hand. We ask it, as always, in Jesus' name. And they all said—"

"Amen."

Click and Garrison spoke in unison, Missus C and Moore a half-beat behind.

Missus C patted Click's hand. "Thank you. It's been a long time since I've had a praying man in the house."

"You been alone now, what?"

"Twenty-six years come next month. My Edwin died just before you went to Korea."

"He was a good man."

"The very best."

While Click and Missus C talked, Garrison laid a hot dog in her bun and scooped on chili and coleslaw. She skipped the onions and mustard for the pickle relish as the final topping. Garrison peered at Moore's hot dog, squinted at the almost invisible squirt of mustard on it. "That's it? You some kind of Yankee?"

Before he could answer, she set her hot dog down and ladled chili and slaw on his.

Moore, when she finished, stared at the conglomeration for the longest time. "You're strange."

"Get used to it."

MOORE and Garrison stood in the doorway, surveying the great front room. It looked so much larger than it was because it had so little in it—a couch, the chair shaped like a hand, the brick-and-board bookcase half full with Moore's library, and the card table.

"You know, I really could put a grand piano in here," Moore said, "even a harp, a harpist, and a string quartet."

She bumped his hip.

He bumped back.

Both giggled like small children at play.

Garrison pulled on a waist-length jacket. "Come on, we better get a tree."

Moore got his sweatshirt and ball cap, and went to the bedroom for gloves. While he was gone, Garrison put on a hat of black fake fur that she had stowed in the sleeve of her jacket.

When he returned, he bent down to kiss her cheek, but thought better of it. They had worked together, off and on for the last months on the Wilson estate and the Taylor murder, she the lawyer, he the investigator. They had shared a supper at the Sunshine Café. They had become friends, good friends, Moore thought. It was she who had put him on to this place.

At the top of the staircase, Garrison put her hand on the banister. "I dare you."

"What, to slide down that? You're nuts."

"Old fud." She got up on the banister, sidesaddle.

"You're going to do it."

"Of course."

"Hey, wait."

"For what?"

"At least let me get down to the bottom to catch you. You crash and break your leg, I've got to explain that to your dad."

Garrison threw her hands up, but she waited while Moore clattered down the stairs. At the bottom, he made a production of bracing himself for the catch of this hundred-thirty-five-pound Tennessee beauty.

She shoved off, arms out, legs out, laughing as if she had no cares at all—down and off the end of the banister into his arms. Moore spun around and fell.

Missus Caudileski dashed into the hallway. "You all right?" she asked when she found Moore and Garrison in a jumble by her front door.

He gazed over Garrison lying across his chest. "Just sliding on the old banister."

"Children, children, children." Missus C took hold of Garrison's arm. She helped her up. "My boys were always doing that."

"Not me. Her," Moore said from the floor.

"Amanda, shame on you. You're a lady."

"So Pop keeps telling me." She straightened her hat before she reached down and helped Moore. "Missus C, haven't you ever slid down that banister?"

The corners of the woman's mouth curled into a smile. "Twice as I remember."

"We're going out to get a Christmas tree. You want to come along?"

"Oh, I already have mine up." She opened the outside door for them. "You two have a good time."

They went out into the chill of the late afternoon, the sun gone, masked by a low deck of slate-gray clouds that had drifted in from the west, clouds that had drifted on beyond Morgantown until the higher reaches of Cullowhee Mountain blocked their passage further to the east. Given time, the clouds would slide up and over the mountain, but snow squalls would hide the movement from human eyes.

The two hunched up as they walked along, their gloved hands stuffed in their pockets. They made the turn at the end of the block and went on to a Christmas tree lot across the street from the Quick Mart. The operator, Holly Clifton, had already turned the lot lights on—a string of bare forty-watters—by the time Garrison and Moore arrived, their breaths crystalline in the air.

Clifton hurried out of the tiny trailer that served as his warming house and office. "Amanda, how you?" the tree seller called out. He pulled the earlappers of his plaid cap down over his earlobes.

"Just fine, Holly. We've come for a tree."

"Yer pap got one a couple weeks ago, didn't he?"

"Yes. This is for—" She tilted her head toward Moore.

Clifton's mittened hand came out. "Holly Clifton," he said.

Moore's gloved hand met Clifton's. "Scott Moore."

"You new here?"

"Guess you could say that. Just moved into the apartment at Missus Caudileski's."

"Oh, that's good. That's a fine place," the tree seller said. "And Missus Caudileski, they don't come no better. I sold her a tree last week."

To Garrison, Clifton fluffed out his beard. "Whatdaya think, Amanda, do I look like Santy Claus?"

"A skinny Santa Claus."

"I got to work more on my eatin'. Well, Mister Moore, let me show you the trees." Clifton led off to the side of the trailer. He studied several trees before he plucked out one. "I only got about a dozen left. They been pretty well picked over, but this un's pretty good."

"Fir, isn't it?" Moore asked.

"Yup, Frasier fir, finest of Christmas trees." Clifton banged the stump on the ground several times. "See? No loose needles."

"How much?"

"Eight dollars."

Moore took off a glove to finger the bills in his pocket. He glanced at the tree and at Garrison, then the other trees, she studying him.

"Why don't we look at the other trees for a moment?" he said.

"Sure, you go right ahead."

Moore nudged Garrison down the line.

"What's the matter?" she whispered.

"I've only got four dollars left, and pay day's not 'til the second."

She put a hand in her jacket pocket and pulled out a bill and some change. She counted. "I've got a dollar and thirty, thirty-five, thirty-seven cents. You're welcome to it."

"You're more broke than I am." He leaned a tree out of the line and gazed at it, put it back, and examined another. He put that one back, too, and pulled out a third.

Disapproval showed on Garrison's face. "It's got a bad side."

"Yes. Maybe he'll let it go cheap." Moore carried the tree over to Clifton, turning it so the tree seller was sure to see the misshapen side, a side that seemed to be missing half its branches. "How much?"

"Can't say I'm proud of that one. You got a corner you can maybe put that bad side in?"

"Maybe."

Clifton rubbed at his shoulder. "Tell you what, I'd take two bucks for it."

"Just a minute." Moore marched away, back down the line. He pulled out a second Scotch pine that could have been a sister to the first. He carried the tree back. "How much for the two of them?"

"You got two corners?"

"Maybe."

"Four dollars."

"Mister Clifton—"

"Call me Holly."

"Holly, these trees aren't likely to sell, are they?"

Clifton traced in the snow with the toe of his boot.

"You're going to have to throw them away after Christmas, aren't you?"

"No, I'll skin the branches off and cut 'em up for firewood."

"What do you say to three dollars for the both of them?"

Clifton continued his tracing. "Three-fifty."

"Three-ten."

"Three-forty."

"Three-twenty."

"Three-twenty, huh?"

"My best offer."

"How about three-thirty? I could maybe go down to three-thirty."

Moore spun the second tree around. "Split the difference."

Clifton glanced up from beneath his eyebrows, a smile exaggerating the crow's feet at the corners of his eyes. "Deal. You got tree stands?"

"Uh-huh." Moore pressed four bills into the tree man's mittened hand. Clifton shucked out three quarters and handed them back. The trooper then worked a hand into the middle of each tree and hefted the butt ends up over his shoulders. "Shall we go?" he said to Garrison.

They started away.

"Amanda?" Clifton called out.

She turned back.

The tree man traced in the snow again, a shy smile showing. "You got a pretty good businessman there."

"Oh, he's not mine."

"Maybe he should be. Speakin' of business, I'm not a young feller anymore. I'm thinkin' maybe I ought to be gettin' a will, maybe one for the missus, too. You bein' a lawyer an' all—"

"I can help you with that."

"That's good. Maybe you'd stop by the house one evening?"

"I'll talk to you tomorrow. We'll find a time."

"Well, you have a good Christmas, and you, too, Mister Moore."

"Scotty."

"Yessir, Scotty. And tell yer friends I still got a few trees left."

It was as if Clifton didn't want to let them go, and at that moment Garrison realized the old tree seller was lonely with so few customers in these last days before Christmas. She wondered what he did in that trailer of his to pass the time. Was he a reader? She didn't know.

"Holly's never cut up a Christmas tree for firewood in his life," she said as she moved along beside Moore and the trees he carried on his shoulders.

"How's that?" he asked.

"Old Holly knows everybody who doesn't have a tree. Christmas Eve, he goes around town, leaving his unsolds on porches. He sets a tree beside a door, knocks, then runs off before anybody can answer."

"And they don't know?"

"Huh-uh."

"Then how do you know?"

"Pop and I saw him one year, when we were coming home from church."

They scuffled on, rounding the corner of the street that led to Missus Caudileski's. Garrison and Moore heard singing. As they got closer, they made out in the gloom of the late afternoon a cluster of people—adults and children—in Missus C's front yard, serenading her.

> *We three kings of Orient are,*
> *bearing gifts we traverse afar—*

"Come on," Garrison said and bumped Moore into a trot.

Field and fountain, moor and mountain
following yonder star—

They cut through someone's front yard and dashed up beside the carolers.

Oh-oo, star of wonder, star of night
star with royal beauty bright
westward leading, still proceeding
guide us to Thy perfect light.

Moore finished with the others, booming along with the carolers.

Several turned to the new voice but saw only greenery next to Garrison.

"Oh, come in, come in," Missus C called to the group, her face radiant. "I've got cookies."

The children stampeded for the porch and the front door, but the adults hung back. A number greeted Garrison, and she introduced Moore, he nodding and speaking from between the trees. The adults, members of the neighborhood Lutheran church, broke away in ones and twos to follow after their children.

Garrison and Moore also went in, only they diverted up the stairs where, at the top, they kicked off their shoes and went inside the flat.

Moore laid the trees down in front of the bay window. He strolled out into the hallway, to the bedroom closet, where he rummaged some and returned with an outsized tree stand in one hand and a toolbox in the other. "We're going to make us one tree," he said.

Garrison laughed.

"You doubt me, wench?"

"Well—"

"Pick up that tree." Moore motioned to the one closest to Garrison.

She hauled it up and held it steady, watching—fascinated—as he mated the other tree to it. Moore wove the branches of the two bad sides together until the tree trunks shouldered against one another.

He took hold of the trees. "I got 'em now. In my toolbox you'll find some picture wire."

"So?"

"So cut me a couple lengths, and I'll tie these trunks together."

Garrison snipped two hanks of wire. She handed them to Moore, and he wrapped them around the trunks, both low and high. He then jammed the trunks into the tree stand. Moore hunkered down onto his belly and reached under the trees, for the bolts in the stand. He turned them in—one, then the other, and the third—while Garrison held the twins straight.

"How's it look?" he asked as he twisted on the last bolt.

She stepped away, then strolled around the mended tree, measuring with her eye how the mated trees stood to vertical. "It's just amazing. Scott, it's amazing. Do you have any lights?"

"Barb got 'em, and I got the ratty tree stand. Some settlement."

A knock came at the door.

"Would you see who that is?" Moore asked as he crawfished out from under the tree. He rolled up on his butt and admired his creation.

Garrison, at the door, opened it. There stood Missus Caudileski with a box wrapped in Christmas paper. "I saw your tree, or should I say trees? Could Mister Scotty use some lights? I got an extra string here."

"Scott?" Garrison asked.

He scrambled to his stockinged feet. "Lights? How did you know?"

"Well, you brought in two trees. I just guessed you might need some extra lights." Missus C peered at the tree in the bay window. "Oh, that's a pretty one. Where'd you put the other?"

"There is no other."

"Pardon?"

"That's it. I put them together."

She went closer and examined the mated trees. She poked around the ends of the branches. "Well, isn't that clever?"

Missus C gave the box to Moore. "You put the lights on, and I'll go down and get some cookies. And I've got the best hot rum punch. I made it for us, not the Lutherans."

She hurried away, out onto the landing and down the stairs.

Garrison swung quarter to Moore. She pursed her lips to restrain a laugh. "How is it having your own grandmother to look after you?"

"You think she'd mend my socks?"

"Don't you dare ask her to do that." She took the box from Moore. "I'll hold this, and you string the lights."

He peered inside. There on top laid something wrapped in tissue paper. Moore lifted it out. With the utmost care, he unwrapped the object and let the paper fall to the floor.

"It's a star," Garrison said.

"And it's got a light in it. Well, this goes on top." Moore went up on his toes. He reached the star high and settling it at the pinnacle of the twin trees. Then he dug into the box for the end of the string of lights. He found it and plugged the star into it. Moore then laid the lights—big Nomas normally reserved for outdoor trees—in among the branches. He and Garrison worked their way around the tree and around again. On the fifth circuit, out came the last of the lights and an extension cord. Moore plugged this into a wall socket.

On came the lights.

Blue lights.

Except for the star. It glowed a soft golden yellow.

Garrison, at the dimmer switch, turned the lights of the chandelier down, then out. She drifted to the center of the room and stood there, gazing at the tree, at the lights, at the star, mesmerized. This is Christmas, she thought. No tinsel, no fake snow, no beribboned boxes elbowing for space beneath the tree. Just sweet silence, the smell of pine, and a tree ever green—the assurance of life.

Moore came up beside her. He slipped his arm around her waist.

She looked up, her gaze meeting his. "Are you going to kiss me?" she asked.

"What?"

She pointed up, to a sprig of mistletoe that hung beneath the chandelier.

Note: I read a slimmed-down version of this story somewhere—I no longer remember where—and thought at the time, boy, the bones for a really good story are here, but the writer just didn't put the needed flesh on them. I did. The result is "Bernie's", a Christmas story that starts in the summertime. Yes, Dorothy, we're in Kansas.

Bernie's

SHE OPENED the coin pouch in her wallet worn thin. Seventy-five cents.

"Goddamn, you, Donnie. Goddamn you to hell."

She closed the pouch, then the wallet, and slipped it into an equally tired shoulder bag. She turned to the six stair-step children clustered around the Formica table, the top abused from age and children's elbows. "Mommy needs to get a job, and I need your help."

"What do you want us to do?" the oldest asked, the girl—Lanny.

"You're all going to have to come with me because I can't leave you home alone. And this isn't a

party we're going to, so you'll have to be extra good."
She gazed down the line. "Any of you have to go to
the bathroom before we leave?"

One of the boys raised his hand, the third
youngest—Emon.

"Lanny, take your brother."

"I don't need no help."

"All right, but don't you dawdle."

The boy shoved off his chair. He went down the
hall while she herded the others out the door.
Outside, she swept the youngest up into her arms as
they walked through the dirt yard to a rusting
Chevrolet. It had been a new car before she had
married—a four-door, a practical gift from her father.

"Alan?" she asked.

"Yeth?"

"Are you all right with this?"

"Whath thith?"

"Mommy getting a job."

"I gueth."

"You're going to have to sit next to Lanny, and
you're going to have to do everything she says."

"Yeth."

She opened the front passenger door and slid the
boy into the center of the seat. Lanny got in beside
him.

She opened a back passenger door. Three boys
scrambled in, ages seven, six, and four. She raised a
finger, and their eyes turned to her. "No slapping. No
pinching. None of this 'he did it to me first.' I didn't
raise you to be little wolves."

The fourth—Emon—squeezed in.

She closed the door and went around to the driver's side. There a brindle mongrel waited, whipping his tail from side to side. She patted his head. "Teddy, you can't come this time. You go over under the trees, all right?"

The tail continued whipping and the eyes remained bright, expectant.

"No, Teddy," she said and pointed off.

The dog's eyes saddened, and his ears and tail drooped. He shambled off as she slipped in behind the steering wheel.

"Why can't Teddy come?" a voice asked from the back.

"It would be too hot for him."

"Can we roll down the windows?"

"Yes, you can roll down the windows."

She twisted the ignition key, and the little six came to life, stuttering. When the engine settled down to a steady rumble, she pushed the column shifter into reverse and backed the car around. She shifted again, into low, and bucked the car across the rutted drive out to the county road where she turned east, toward Manhattan.

"Where's Daddy?" a voice asked from the back.

She glanced up at the reflections in the rearview mirror. "Gone."

"For good?"

"Yes. I think so."

"Good. I didn't like him. He hit me."

"He hit all of us."

"Why'd he do that?"

"I don't know."

A new voice came from the back. "Mommy, why do you need a job?"

"Because we need money for food and rent."

"I thought that's what Daddy was for."

"He's not going to help us anymore."

"Oh. . . . Can I get a job?"

"Nathan, I'm afraid you're too little."

Shoot for the top her father had always told her. In Manhattan, that would be the Wareham Hotel, so she guided the Chevrolet up Blumont Hill and down the other side, through the college district and Aggieville before she cut over to Poyntz, the main business street. She nudged the car into a parking place across from the hotel and the county courthouse.

She got out and leaned back in the open window. "When I come out, I don't want to hear one complaint. Not one, do you understand? This is important. You listen to Lanny. She's in charge."

She brushed the wrinkles from the one dress she owned as she crossed the street. She glanced at the luster on her leather shoes, adjusted her bag on her shoulder, brushed back her hair, and went on inside, through the oversized glass doors that were, with the arched and rococo overhang, the mark of the Wareham.

"Elaine Mars," she said to the man at the desk. "Who do I see about getting a job?"

He snapped his fingers at the maitre d'.

The tuxedoed gentleman responded. He swept across the lobby. "Oscar Brown," the man said. "May I help you?"

Such attention. For a moment Elaine lost control of her voice, but managed to generate an "I-need-a-job-I-can-wait-tables."

The maitre d' stepped back. He appraised the woman. "I'm sorry, we only use men on our wait staff."

"I can bus tables."

"Only men."

"I can cook. I have six children."

"I doubt you cook the kind of cuisine we serve."

"Wash dishes?"

"No openings."

"Housekeeping? I can make beds, clean rooms."

"Full up. Have you tried the college?"

"I've heard you pay better."

"I'm sure we do. If you would be willing to leave your telephone number?"

"I don't have a telephone."

"Then I am indeed sorry."

She left and went across the street to Baker's Department Store. She struck out there, and at the Murphy Five & Dime, the office supply store, the flower shop, and the newspaper office. Business offices were out of the question for she had never learned to type. But a woman reporter at the newspaper, walking out the door with her, offered a glimmer of hope.

"I've got kids of my own," the reporter said. "You know the Root Beer Barrel Drive-In on Eighteen, out by the airport? Somebody's bought it, added onto it, and put in gas pumps. It's a truck stop now and restaurant. They may not be all hired up yet."

Elaine wanted to touch the woman, squeeze her hand, say thank you. Instead she teared up.

"Hard day, huh?"

"Yes."

"I'll say a prayer for you."

The walk back to the car, though only four blocks, seemed to be the longest in the world. She knew her children would be hungry, but with only seventy-five cents . . . and she couldn't afford to drive out to Keats and make lunch for them, then back into town and out onto Eighteen.

In the car came that voice from the backseat. "I gotta pee."

"Nathan, can you hold it for five minutes more?"

"I can try."

Elaine herded the car into a Standard station, to a gas pump. A mechanic trotted out, wiping his hands on a shop rag.

"A quarter's worth. And can we use your restroom?" she asked.

He twisted the gas cap off the filler tube. "Right around the end there. You'll find it."

Off Elaine marched, Alan in her arms, the rest strung out like a gaggle of goslings.

She went into the "Women's" with Alan. While Elaine supervised him, she splashed her face with water, then dried herself on the towel that hung from the towel machine. Alan done, she pushed him out and hauled in the next, and so it went.

"You have no idea how hard it is being the mother of six when they all have to go to the bathroom," she said after she placed a quarter in the mechanic's grease-stained hand.

"Lady, that's why God invented gas stations. You sure you can afford that half-gallon of gas?"

"Do I have a choice? I got to get out to the Root Beer Barrel and get me a job."

"It's Bernie's now."

"What?"

"The place. It's called Bernie's now. If you get on there, you can get gas there at a discount."

SHE PARKED in front of the plate glass window on which someone had painted the outline of a semi and, on the side of the trailer, "Bernie's." Beneath the name, "Open 24 Hours."

"No monkey business while I'm inside," she said to the boys in the backseat. "See that window? I can see you from inside."

Her instruction delivered, Elaine got out of the car. Once more she brushed the wrinkles from her dress. She hurried inside, the air pungent with the aromas of barbecue, strong coffee, and sweet pie. Was it cherry? "I need a job," she said to the woman washing the counter.

The woman, older than Elaine, in a white uniform dress with lambchop sleeves, set her cleaning rag aside. She rescued a cigarette from the lip of an ashtray and took a drag as she eyed the person in front of her. Without so much as a hello, she called over her shoulder, "Bernie!"

"Yup?" came a whiskey tenor voice from the kitchen.

"Girl out here wants a job."

"Tell her to keep her panties on."

The woman gestured to a stool, and Elaine sat down.

"Coffee?"

"I don't think so. Water would be all right."

The woman glanced out the window at the car as she scooped a glass into an ice bucket under the counter. She finished by filling the glass with water from a metal pitcher and set the glass before Elaine. "Those your kids out there?"

"Yes."

"That why you need a job?"

"Uh-huh."

"How many?"

"Six."

"Nice." She flicked ash from her cigarette into the ashtray. "I got three myself. One married and away, one in the Army in Germany, one be a senior in high school come fall. They do grow up fast." She sucked again on her cigarette. "So let me guess, you're on your own."

Elaine did not answer.

A stout woman in a grease- and food-stained dress and armed with a scrubbing block hustled in through the swinging doors that separated the diner from the kitchen. She wore a K-State baseball cap at a rakish angle over her close-cropped gray hair. "Megs," she asked, "this the girl?"

Elaine stood before the waitress could answer. She held tight to her bag as she said, "I'm Elaine Mars, and I can do anything that needs doing around a diner."

"Uh-huh. Got any experience?"

"I've cooked and cleaned for six kids and a husband."

Megs Randall, the waitress, turned to move away, to take an order from a trucker at the end of the counter. She whispered to Bernie as she went past, "Husband left her."

Bernie's eyebrows knit together, shaping up a furrow between them. "Wash dishes?"

"Anything."

"I got one job open, honey. Dishwasher on the graveyard shift."

"Are you offering it to me?"

"Only if you can start tonight."

The widest smile that would warm even a banker's heart brought new life to Elaine's face. "I'll take it," she said. "What time should I be here?"

AS PROMISED, Elaine Mars came through the door of Bernie's Truck Stop & Diner at eleven-thirty. She wore jeans, a checked shirt, and had her auburn hair tied back in a ponytail.

Bernie, sucking on a cup of coffee at a corner table, waved her over. "Sit and let's talk. You get something to eat before you came in?"

"Supper with the kids."

"That's, what, six hours ago?"

As Elaine sat down, Bernie let out a whistle that had the volume of Gabriel's trumpet. In response, a man's face appeared above the swinging doors.

"Robert," she said, "scrambled eggs and sausage here, Texas toast. . . . You want coffee with that, honey?"

"Milk, but I really don't have any money—"

Bernie turned again to her cook. "Milk with that."

He waved and disappeared.

Bernie leaned back in her chair. "Honey, the work here's hard and the pay's poor—sixty-five cents an hour. I'll stake you to three meals a shift as long as you keep them cheap."

"I don't eat much."

"I can see that. You're on the skinny side. Skinny employees is no recommendation for a diner, so I want to see you get some meat on those bones."

"Mind if I ask a question?"

"Shoot."

"Do I really call you Bernie?"

"It's Bernice Dawson, but only my mother ever called me Bernice."

Robert-the-cook, balding beneath his paper cap tipped forward, clomped out from the kitchen. He dropped a plate of scrambled eggs and sausage, and eating utensils rolled in a paper napkin in front of Elaine. "Toast be up in a minute," he said and left before she could get out a thank you.

Bernie motioned for her to eat. "That's about the most you're gonna hear from Robert. He comes off as a mean sonuvabitch, but if he likes you—" She gave a thumbs-up.

Elaine tried the eggs. "This is good," she said, pointing her fork at her plate.

"Old Robert does things with herbs I'd never think of. Shame he's gotten himself thrown out of every restaurant from Wamego to Junction City."

Elaine cut a bite of sausage. "Is it all right to ask why?"

"You'd find out sometime. He tends to pop off to management and at the worst times."

"You?"

Bernie laughed. "Some diner people keep a pistol under the cash register. I keep a Little League baseball bat. Robert popped off to me one night, so I laid him out. He's never argued since."

The cook reappeared. He dropped a saucer of buttered toast on the table and left.

"Robert! Milk for the lady."

"Right."

Elaine bit into the toast.

"Honey, when you get back in the kitchen," Bernie said, "you're gonna find a pile of dishes waiting for you. My afternoon dishwasher goes off at eight, so from eight to midnight, the dishes accumulate. You get that mountain done, then you clean the kitchen, and I mean you scrub it, everything except the grill and the ovens. That's Robert's, and you don't mess with his area. Morning cook comes in at six—that's Earlene Hobbs—and I'll tell you now, everything had better be right or she's gonna fan your ears. Cleanliness and order isn't next to godliness. For Earlene, it is godliness."

The cook appeared a third time. Before he could drop the glass, Bernie swiped it from his hand. "You are a gentleman, aren't you, Robert?"

"I guess."

"This is Elaine Mars, your dishwasher."

"Right. You tell her to leave my grill alone?"

"That I did."

"You tell her I don't like talk?"

"Think she figured that out."

"Right."

Bernie waved toward the kitchen, and Robert-the-cook left. She sipped her coffee, then set her cup aside. "You dry your dishes?"

Elaine, her mouth full of scramble egg, nodded.

"We don't here. Your rinse water, I want that scalding hot. China comes out of that, they'll dry themselves in a minute if you don't pack them tight. Glasses, though, I want you to hand-dry them, I mean polish them. Knives, forks, spoons, you'll have to dry them, too."

"Pots and pans?"

"Got a separate sink for those. You see Robert sling something your way, you quit whatever you're doing, rake it out, and wash it right then. He may not need that pan for a couple hours, but you never make him wait. You stay ahead of him, he's a happy man. You ready to go in there?"

Elaine gulped down her milk. She set the glass aside and levered herself out of her chair.

Bernie gestured at the dishes. "Bring those with you."

Elaine stacked them. She followed along, pausing before the swinging doors, timing them, then shot through before they could whump her. She stepped into the third ring of hell, the kitchen horribly hot, but the smell was not of scorched flesh but of bread. Robert-the-cook opened one of his ovens as Elaine went by. He took from it a sheet on which six loaves of bread rested in their pans, the loaves done, their golden top crusts mounded high. He set the sheet aside, picked up a second sheet with six bread pans on it, and shoved it in the oven.

Bernie, at the sink, had the hot water running by the time Elaine caught up. Steam roiled up, giving the impression the stainless steel sink was a witch's cauldron.

"Dish detergent and your cleaning supplies are on the shelf there," Bernie said, motioning to the side. She picked up a rubber scraper as wide as a plate. "Use this to get all the slop off. One swipe across a plate over the garbage can. Can gets full, you take it out back and bring in another."

She tossed the scraper aside and pulled over a blue plastic tub. "Your dry dishes you stack in tubs like this. Glasses, cups, saucers, dessert plates, and silverware you carry out to the diner. Tibby will show you where she wants them. She's my graveyard waitress." Bernie waved toward the grill and the prep table. "Plates and bowls go on the counter over there for Robert. Put the pots and pans there, too. He'll stow them tonight until you figure out where he wants them. Starting tomorrow night, you put them away. Questions?"

Elaine swiped her sleeve at the sweat beading out on her forehead. "Cleaning the kitchen?"

"You work your way through that mountain of dishes, Robert will tell you what to do. Listen close and memorize. He won't tell you anything a second time. 'Nuther question?"

"Drying towels?"

"Drawer behind you. Anything else?"

"Guess not."

"Good. Tomorrow night, honey, wear a tee-shirt. It's too damn hot in here for long sleeves." Bernie held out a pair of rubber gloves with shanks long enough to reach to a person's elbows. "You wear these or you'll boil your hands. And your hair."

"What about my hair?"

"Health regs. You wear a hair net or a cap."

"I don't have a hair net."

Bernie handed over her K-State ball cap. "Then you wear this. I got another at home."

Elaine put the cap on and the gloves. She reached for the bottle of dish detergent.

"You all have a good time," Bernie said and moved away. "See you tomorrow night."

Elaine watched her while she shot some soap in the water. Suds mounded up. She swung the faucet over the rinse sink, to let the hot water run there. Scraper, dirty dishes, garbage can . . . from the corner of her eye Elaine saw Bernie leaning into Robert, Robert brushing melted butter over the crusts of the bread that had come from the oven. *What's she telling him? She's pointing at me.*

A plate twisted from her hand. She grabbed for it, didn't catch it, instead knocked it further away, and it fell to the concrete floor—the sound like unemployment, chunks of china skittering.

Bernie hustled back. She scooped up the largest piece and held it in front of Elaine, her face frozen in horror. "I'll give you this one, sweets. Next one, and any after that, comes out of your pay."

She tossed the evidence of carelessness in the garbage can and left by way of the swinging doors.

Elaine went down on her knees. She gathered the big pieces and put them in the trash, leaving the bits and slivers to be swept up later. Water splashing on the floor interrupted, hot-hot water boiling over the rim of the rinse sink.

ELAINE BENT over the garbage can, stripping gobs of dough from a dough hook. Robert-the-cook, drying his hands on his apron, kicked her foot.

H thumbed toward the diner. "Break time."

Elaine tossed the hook in the wash water. She shed a glove. "What time is it?"

"Four-oh-two."

She pulled off her other glove, threw it aside, and swept back a sweat-soaked strand of hair. "I'm dead, Robert."

"Then get outta my kitchen before you stink."

"You're real sweetness, know that?" She swiped her hands through the wash water and, as she slouched out of the kitchen, dried them on a dish towel. Elaine pushed through the swinging doors to see Tibby Watson sitting at a table, smoking, waving to her.

"You gonna make it through the night?" Tibby asked.

Elaine slumped into a chair. "I thought looking after six kids was hard work, with all the cooking, cleaning, and laundry. And bath time."

"Two hours, you can go home."

A trucker at the counter, stirring a stream of sugar into his coffee, glanced in the direction of the table. "Who's the new kid, Tibby?"

"Elaine Mars." The graveyard waitress blew a lungful of smoke toward a ceiling fan lazily stirring the air. "Elaine, the hunk there is Eddie Wilson. Drives for Humphrey. Guy at the pinball machine is J.D. Castro, 'nuther Humphrey driver. Whatcha hauling, Eddie?"

"Blue jeans from a sewing factory in Tennessee to California."

"J.D., too?"

"Drums of grease."

"We see 'em every couple weeks."

"You married, Elaine?" Wilson asked.

"Kinda."

"Too bad. If you were single, I might sweet talk ya into ridin' along with J.D. He's single."

Castro fired a new ball into the game. He watched the ball ping off pins and bumpers and catch a chute that carried it toward a star burst and big points, but a spinner whipped the ball away. Castro slammed the flat of his hand against the machine.

Wilson sampled his coffee. He grimaced and poured another stream of sugar in.

Tibby pointed her cigarette at him. "You making syrup there, Eddie?"

"Yeah, yeah, yeah."

Robert-the-cook appeared beside the table. He dropped a platter with a hamburger and hash fries on it in front of Elaine. "Bernie says you're supposed to eat. You want milk with that, you know where it is. You get it yourself."

He humped away to a far table. There he pulled a paperback and a pouch of raisins from his back pocket before he threw a leg across a chair. Robert-the-cook read and popped raisins.

The bell over the front door jingled. All ignored it, if they heard it. A man in tans and a cowboy hat, a star pinned above his breast pocket, and a pistol on his hip came in. "Mornin', all," he said and went behind the counter. There the deputy sheriff helped himself to a heavy china mug. He filled it from the Buns machine, all the while glancing in the mirror at the images of Tibby and Elaine. "Somebody new here, Aunt Tib?"

The waitress took another drag on her cigarette. To Elaine, she said, "My nephew."

The deputy grabbed up a fresh cinnamon roll before he came over. "Bailey Devlon," he said as he sat down. He shoved his hat onto the back of his head revealing a scar just below his hairline.

Tibby aimed the glowing end of her cigarette at the deputy's hat. "Don't you ever take that off?"

"Only when I go to bed." Bailey winked at Elaine working on her burger.

"Elaine Mars," Tibby said. "She's as married as you are. Six kids."

Bailey took a bite from his cinnamon roll. "I got three and a fourth on the way."

Tibby stubbed out her cigarette. "My nephew is a good person to know. He'll tote your groceries, fix a sick car. Last winter—now you might think this is bragging, but this is true—Bailey got Wally Smith, the road grader operator up by Leonardville, to plow a trail through the drifts to the Morton ranch, and he hauled the old man to the hospital with lights and sirens. Old Horace got himself busted up by his bull."

Bailey blew across his coffee, cooling it. "Hey, I just look after the people who elect my boss." To Elaine, he asked, "You vote Republican, ma'am?"

"Last time, yes."

"You won't go wrong there."

Robert-the-cook appeared at Elaine's elbow, book in hand. "Bailey," he said.

The deputy raised his coffee mug in a salute.

Robert slapped his book against the side the table. "Mars, break's over. Let's get at it."

Elaine picked up her platter and silverware as she stood, and Tibby put her cup and saucer on the platter. "Good to meet you, Deputy—"

"Bailey. Bailey Devlon."

She gave him a tentative smile as she turned away. Again she timed the swing of the doors and shot through to the kitchen. When she arrived at the sink, there stood Robert-the-cook wagging his book at the garbage can.

"Best get that outside and get a fresh one in here." Message delivered, he went to the cooler.

Elaine grasped the can's handles.

She jerked up.

The can came up and as quickly went down, hitting the floor so hard globs of gravy splashed up onto Elaine's face and shirt.

"Problem?" Robert asked as he came by with a box of bacon.

She raked the back of her hand at the gravy on her cheek. "This is too heavy."

"You shouldn'tna filled it so full."

"Nobody told me. Will you help me?"

"Not my job. If you can't lift it, drag it." He plunged a butcher knife into the top of the box and sawed it open.

Elaine eyed the can. She wrapped the fingers of both hands around one handle and lifted, pulled. The can scraped a couple inches on the edge of its bottom.

Lift/pull, life/pull, she scrunched backwards toward the screen door that led to the world outside, the world behind the diner, the garbage can following. Elaine felt her butt against the screen and heard the hinges squall as she backed through the doorway.

Her heel caught on the sill, the can in mid-slide.

Elaine spilled over backwards.

The can came with her—tipping, falling, its contents flooding out into her lap.

"Robert!"

ELAINE HUNCHED over her kitchen table, counting her week's pay into envelopes—rent, groceries, electric, school supplies, kids' clothes, gas, doctor, Christmas. Nothing went into the Christmas envelope or the kids' clothes envelope, and precious little into the doctor's. If the kids stayed healthy through the fall, maybe she could chip away at the doctor's bill.

An exhausted teenager, her hair in pin curls and an algebra book in the crook of her arm, pushed through the outside door. "Sorry to be late, Missus Mars, but Mom and Dad just got home. I couldn't leave my little brother."

"That's all right. The kids have been asleep." Elaine scooped the envelopes into an oatmeal box. She glanced at the clock above the kitchen sink as she tucked the box away on the top shelf of her cupboard. "I've still got a half an hour. I should be able to make it to work on time."

"Is it all right if I study in the kitchen? If I have the light on in the front room, it might wake them."

"That's fine."

The girl—Debbie Gibbs—opened her book as she sat down. Elaine had worked a deal with her to be with the children from eleven at night to six-thirty in the morning, a no-strain babysitting job because Elaine's children were asleep. "You can sleep on the couch," she had said. "It's just important that you be here."

A dollar a night, almost two hours of her pay.

Elaine peered in the big room where the children slept in three beds. The smallest three boys had kicked off their sheet, so she pulled it up, taking time to touch each one on the cheek before she left.

Back in the kitchen, she gathered up her wallet and keys from the counter and went outside to the car. Gracie she called it. Faithful, but it had been getting harder to start, and the old girl's brakes squealed. One of the truckers said that meant the car needed new brake pads and maybe the drums turned. It was an expense Elaine didn't need.

She pumped on the gas pedal before she keyed the ignition. "Come on now, come on," Elaine said as she turned the key. The starter ground away. Elaine held the key in and pumped more on the gas pedal, and the cylinders fired.

The drive in from Keats to Manhattan went by without event—no one on the road at that hour, although a pair of glistening eyes watched from the grass in the ditch as she guided Gracie around a bend. A cat out hunting, Elaine figured. She jogged south on Seventeenth Street to Highway Eighteen and headed west out of town.

As she rounded Sunset Hill, she saw the beacon at the airport, turning, rotating—a nightly presence, always there. Comforting.

A shot and Gracie's front end shook with the violence of a mad machine flinging parts of itself away. Elaine, her eyes as large as dinner plates, clung to the steering wheel. She rode the brake pedal, the brakes howling.

When Gracie had slowed enough, Elaine worked the car off onto the shoulder, the shaking slowing to a thumping bounce on the right.

She turned the engine off, but left the headlights on. Her fingers ached from holding so tight to the steering wheel—real white knuckles. She massaged them as she forced herself out of the car. Whatever it was . . . whatever it was, Elaine discovered when she came around front, was a flat tire. The right front.

"Gracie, how could you?" Elaine kicked at the gravel. "I don't have time for this."

Change the tire or walk the mile to Bernie's, which would be faster? She couldn't afford to be late.

Well . . .

Elaine went back to the driver's door. She pulled the ignition key and trudged back to the trunk. She opened it, not quite as dark as a coal mine, and felt around for the tire iron, the jack, and the spare. The spare, something about it didn't feel right. Elaine pushed on it, and the tire gave, gave too much. Had it gone flat?

She wanted to cry, wanted to beat on Gracie with the tire iron, wanted to . . .

Headlights came around Sunset, and a red light flashing. The car—a sheriff's cruiser—slowed. It pulled over onto the shoulder and rolled to a stop behind Gracie.

"Trouble?" a voice asked.

Elaine shaded her eyes from the glare of the headlights. "That you, Bailey?"

"Mighty Mouse here to save the world."

"Tire blew out. And my spare's flat."

The deputy, wearing his ever-present cowboy hat, came forward into the lights. "Makes you want to spit, doesn't it? We can put my spare on. Oh hell, we can't do that. Ford has a different lug bolt pattern than Chevy."

"What am I going to do?"

"Ride with me, I guess. I'll drop you at the truck stop, but that's still gonna leave you with a car with two dead tires. Tell you what, get the jack out."

"Is this going to make me late?"

"Hey, I got pull with management. Tibby's my aunt, remember?"

Bailey grubbed a couple rocks out of the ditch and blocked the three good wheels. When Elaine brought him the jack and tire iron, he rammed the jack under the frame and ran it up enough to begin lifting the right front corner of the car. Bailey wrenched the wheel cover off, and he broke the five lug nuts free, each in turn, and spun them off.

"I crew for a buddy who drives stocks on the dirt track up at Clay," Bailey said as he ratcheted the jack up. "Nobody faster at changing a tire than me."

He pulled the flat off and threw it in the backseat of his cruiser. In the light from the dome, he gazed at the tire. He ran his hand over the tread. "Jeez, Elaine, this is a skin. Your others this bald?"

"I don't know. I never look."

Bailey rescued his flashlight from the front seat. He marched around Gracie, shining a beam on the tread of each of the remaining tires. He shook his head as he came back around. He turned off the car's headlights, rolled up the driver's window, and waved Elaine toward the passenger seat of his cruiser.

Inside, Bailey noted the time of his stop on a log sheet.

Elaine twisted around. "Why's your car smell so bad?"

"A drunk threw up his guts in the backseat. I hosed it out as best I could."

"You should get one of those pine trees to hang on your mirror. We have some by the cash register."

"I was thinking about that." He made a couple more notes. "Here's what I can do. In the morning, I can take you home. We'll drop that baldy at the Mobile station. Maybe Ernie can fix it."

"Bailey, I don't have any money for that."

"Well, sometimes Ernie does favors. Anyway, I'll pick up the tire when I come on tomorrow night, drive you to your car, put the tire on, and you're back in business until the next one busts."

"Maybe it won't."

Bailey swung his cruiser back out onto the highway. "We do live on hope, don't we?"

TIBBY CHECKED her watch: four-ten. She pulled a new stick from her pack of Camels and lit it.

Elaine worked at putting down a fried-egg sandwich. "I don't know what I'm going to do, Tib," she said. "Two flat tires and Bailey says my others won't last long."

Eddie Wilson turned from his peach pie at the counter. "Flat tire, you say?"

Tibby waggled two fingers, her cigarette between them.

"I'm haulin' a load of that new Fix-a-Flat stuff. Lemme go out to the truck, an' I'll getcha a couple cans."

Elaine held onto the remnant of her sandwich. "Eddie, I don't have any money."

"Tonight it's free. There's always something falling off a load. They never miss it at the warehouse."

The bell rang over the front door.

Bailey Devlon came in. He went behind the counter and filled a china mug from the Buns. He also helped himself to a second mug. This one he banged down in front of Eddie. "I'm taking up a collection. Put two bucks in there."

"Why the hell should I?"

Bailey leaned his hand on the butt of his pistol. "So you don't get a ticket when you go out to your truck."

"Why would I get a ticket?"

"I'm sure I can find a reason. You heard about Elaine's flat tire?"

"Yeah."

"It's worse than flat. I checked it over, and she busted a sidewall. Gonna need a whole new tire. Your money?"

Eddie pulled a long black wallet from his back pocket, the wallet chained to a belt loop. He excavated deep within the wallet's innards until he found two one-dollar bills. Eddie stuffed them in the cup.

Bells went off at the pinball machine. J.D. Castro, Eddie's driving partner, whooped and did his version of the monkey. "Ten thousand! I dare anybody to beat that."

Bailey ambled over. He stuck his money mug under the nose of the happy driver. "Three bucks since you're feeling so good. Ante up, J.D."

Castro put in a fistful of nickels, but snatched one out. That he dropped into the slot in the front of the pinball machine and waited for a line of balls to roll out for a new game.

Bailey went to the back table where Robert-the-cook sat engrossed in a paperback. "What you readin' tonight, Robert?"

He didn't look up. He turned a page. "Proust."

"He as good a writer as Zane Grey?"

Robert-the-cook ignored that.

"Put some money in the cup, pilgrim."

Robert grubbed a wrinkled one from his watch pocket.

"Your generosity is underwhelming, but I thank you." Bailey took the bill and went on to the women's table. He pulled out a chair, and, as he sat, he slid the money cup in front of Tibby. "Your tip money, Aunt Tib. All of it in there."

She emptied the pocket of her apron and dropped the contents in the mug. "Haven't seen you put any money in."

Bailey took a wad from his side pocket. He counted it out. "Two bucks from our other night deputy. Dollar thirty-eight from our dispatcher—that's all she had. And two bucks and a dime from me, the dime I was gonna pay for my coffee." He raked it all toward Elaine, she astonished.

"I can't take this," she said.

Bailey drummed his fingers on the table top. "We didn't ask you, so it's not something you can turn down. If there's not enough there for the new tire, we'll dicker with Ernie and get the price knocked down."

HEADLIGHTS flashed through the side window of Elaine's kitchen, from a car turning into her driveway.

"That your ride, Missus Mars?" Debbie Gibbs asked from the table where she worked at a string of algebra equations.

Elaine, in clean jeans and a tee-shirt, glanced out the window. She hurried toward the door, but turned back. "I get paid tonight, so I can pay you in the morning, even catch you up for last week when I was short. Is that all right?"

"I never worry, Missus Mars. This is the easiest money I make."

"All right then, see you in the morning."

She went on outside and down to the driveway where a sheriff's cruiser was parked, idling, the passenger door open.

Bailey Devlon sat listening to his radio, a woman's voice coming from the speaker. "Got a disturbance up by Randolph. Who's closer?"

The deputy squeezed the transmitter button on his microphone. "I'm in Keats."

A man's voice came back. "I'm on the plateau at Twenty-Four and Seventy-Seven. I'll take it."

Dispatcher: "Caller says it's at the third house up from the bank. If it's a domestic and you need help, call me and I'll send Bailey up."

"Roger that."

Bailey squeezed the transmit button again. "I'm going over to Eighteen to get a car back on the road. From there I'll go hang around Fort Riley, see if I can catch some drunk soldiers weavin' on the road."

Dispatcher: "This that dishwasher's car?"

"The same."

"Get the new tire?"

"Yup."

"Very good."

Elaine closed the door.

Bailey threw the cruiser into reverse and backed out onto the county road. He tickled the pine tree hanging from his rearview mirror as he shifted into drive. "Like it?"

"It improves the air."

"Your new tire is in the backseat."

"Was there enough money?"

Bailey pulled an envelope from his pocket and held it out. "Old Ern was having a half-price sale. Enough money left so maybe you can buy new shoes for one of your kids."

"I really need to buy new jeans for the boys. I've been patching patches to keep them going." Elaine took the envelope. She squeezed it and felt a mass of coins and how many bills she couldn't tell. "You know, I still owe the doctor some from last summer."

"It's always something, isn't it?"

"It never lets up. It was easier when my husband was around."

Bailey glanced over. "Aunt Tib told me you've been on your own for a while. Maybe Bernie will move you out front as a waitress. The tip money would help, plus the hourly pay's probably better."

"It would be. . . . Do you like what you do?"

Bailey turned back to his driving, slowing as they rolled into Manhattan. "Most nights it's seven and a half hours of boredom and five minutes of panic, and you never know what the panic is gonna be about—a speeder, some old drunk guy who's put his car in the ditch and wants to fight you when you have to haul him in, a burglar from Topeka who thinks he's gonna have easy pickin's over here. Some of them don't want to be caught."

He turned onto Seventeenth Street and drove on in silence to the highway going west.

"You?" Bailey asked. "You always lived around here?"

"I'm from Junction. Been here for two years."

They rounded Sunset Hill, and Bailey flipped on his bubble light. The revolving flash and his headlights picked up Elaine's car still parked on the shoulder of the road. Bailey pulled up behind and stopped. He handed Elaine his flashlight. "Take this and check your car over, make sure you didn't get any dings while it was out here. I'll get this tire on for you."

"Do you need help?"

"I'm a big boy."

Elaine slid out of the cruiser. She pushed the flashlight switch to on as she walked toward her car, but no light showed. She slapped the flashlight into her hand once, twice, and a beam shot forward. Elaine played it over the back of Gracie. Nothing out of place. She went on to the side and moved the beam across the door panels and the fenders—fine. Then she aimed the light through the glass of the side window.

Surprise lightened her face. "Bailey?"

"What?"

"Did you do this?"

He came up, the new tire and wheel rim under his arm. "Do what?"

She pointed the light through the side window. "There are one, two, three, four tires in the backseat."

Bailey leaned in for a better look. "Damn, they look new. Well, this has got to be a first, a break-in where the burglar leaves something rather than takes something."

"I asked you, did you do this?"

"Hell no. It's a bit early, but maybe you've got a secret Santa Claus."

ELAINE, wielding a steel brush, scrubbed her way down into a mashed-potatoes pot that could have seen service in an Army mess kitchen. As she scrubbed, she huffed a breath up through an extended lower lip, to dislodge a strand of sweaty hair that had fallen onto her face. She came up for air and, irritated, raked the strand to the side with the back of her hand.

Robert-the-cook sauntered by, carrying a tray of pies he'd taken from the oven. He peered into the pot. "Missed some there," he said and walked on.

"I know. I'm not finished yet."

"That's for certain. I'm gonna roll out the last of the dough for elephant ears, and you can have the mixing bowl to clean up next."

"Robert, I don't know how to thank you."

She again attacked the pot only to hear the graveyard waitress, Tibby Watson, clearing her throat. Elaine glanced up.

The woman leaned an elbow across the swinging doors, a cigarette in her fingers. "Telephone for you."

Elaine grabbed up a dish towel. "Nobody ever calls me."

"Until tonight, sweetie. She says she's your babysitter."

"If this is about Emon throwing up—I've got three kids down with colds."

"There's a lot of that going around."

Elaine dried her hands as she pushed out through the swinging doors into the diner, to the wall phone behind the cash register. She waved her dish towel to the night deputy, Bailey Devlon, sitting at the counter in his cowboy hat and sheepskin winter jacket. He gave an easy wave without breaking his conversation with someone in coveralls hunched over a cup of coffee.

She rescued the handset and put it to her ear. "Debbie, if it's Emon—"

"It isn't, Missus Mars," came a teenage girl's voice from a distance, panic seeping through. "It's Lanny. She's crying."

"She never cries."

"Her forehead's as hot as a stove and her stomach hurts something awful, she says. I don't know what to do."

"Oh Lord. Listen, Debbie, here's what you do. You put cold wash cloths on Lanny's forehead, you hear? That ought to help on her fever, but her stomach I don't know. I guess I'll have to come home."

"I've never seen anyone this sick."

"Colds can be awful bad."

"But what if it isn't a cold?"

"I guess then we'll have to get her to a doctor."

"It's snowing out there, Missus Mars."

"Debbie, it's the middle of December. It does that. Now hang up and get those cold wash cloths."

A click came across the line.

Elaine hung the handset back on its cradle. When she turned around, worry showed in deep trenches across her forehead. "Tib, I gotta go home."

"Figured that from your half of the conversation."

"I have a really sick kid. I have to go."

"With this snow coming down, you might as well. We're not going to have anyone else in before breakfast, if then. But you be careful."

Elaine hurried to the wall hooks where her mackinaw hung among a cluster of other coats. She pulled her mack down and stuffed her arms into its sleeves. While she buttoned herself in, a shadow came close—Bailey Devlon.

He stood nearby, his hands in his back pockets. "You got snow chains?"

"Snow chains?"

"Yeah, it's got kinda deep out there since you come on. A couple hours ago, I had to trade my cruiser for the sheriff's four-wheel drive, you know, to buck the drifts on the county roads."

Elaine paused in cinching a knit cap down over her ears. "I don't have chains."

"Why am I not surprised as church-mouse poor as you are. Look, I couldn't help but hear you've got a sick child. I'll drive you out to Keats 'cause you're not gonna get there with that car of yours."

"Bailey, I can do this."

"No, you can't."

"Yes, I can."

"Don't get stubborn on me."

"I'm not getting stubborn on you."

"Yes, you are."

"Oh all right, but we better go."

He detoured back to the counter with Elaine, to the person in coveralls he'd been talking to. "Elaine, this fella is Wally Smith, runs that big road grader out in the lot for the county."

The graderman gave a wave that showed three fingers missing from his right hand.

"Wall, you been out on the Keats road tonight?"

"Not yet."

Bailey grimaced as he moved the toe of his boot around the grit on the floor. "This woman's got a sick child out there. I suppose my fastest way to get her home isn't the main roads, is it, but the old ranch road across country."

"Wind's out of the north, so I'd say most of it should be blowed free of snow. Still you gotta ford the Wildcat."

"I've got the sheriff's Power Wagon."

"Then I'd say go for it."

The two went on outside, Elaine shocked that what had been a skiff of snow before midnight was well up over her ankles and the drift she stepped in twice, if not three times as deep. Snow swirled down off the roof of the diner, coating her and Bailey. He yanked open the passenger door for her and helped her up the step and into the cab of the tall pickup, the cab smelling of moist, sweet tobacco. The handle of a shovel poked up in the back window and a logging chain laid in a jumble on the floor, a coffee can and a pouch of Red Man among the litter on the seat.

Bailey slammed the door and came around to the driver's side where he pulled himself up and in. "Pardon the mess. It's the sheriff's, not mine," he said as he twisted the key in the ignition.

The engine came to life with a roar. "George put the biggest V-Eight he could find under the hood to make this his go-anywhere truck. You hang on now."

He backed away from the diner, then aimed the truck out of the lot and onto the airport road, the snow flying horizontal at a dizzying speed through the shafts of light from the truck's headlamps. At the end of the road, two-hundred yards on, Bailey bucked the truck off to the north, toward the bluffs that separated the airport valley from the Wildcat Valley, the bluffs lost in the night and the snow.

Bailey recovered a microphone from the mess to the side of him. He squeezed the transmit button. "Dispatch, you on?"

A woman's voice came through the speaker on the truck's dashboard. "I'm here."

"I'm leaving Bernie's, going cross-country to Keats. One civilian on board."

"The Mars woman?"

"You got it. She's got a sick child and we got to get her home. Ronnie out there?"

"He's up at Randolph. He decided to wait out the storm at his cousin's place."

"So I'm it if something goes wrong, huh?"

"You get to be the hero."

"Thanks. Devlon out."

He tossed the microphone aside as the truck began its climb upward, jolting from rock to chuckhole, the transmission whining.

Elaine grabbed for the handhold above the passenger door. "We're alone, huh?"

"Appears so."

"I didn't know there was a road here."

Bailey held to the steering wheel shaking in his hands. "Abandoned."

"Guess I have to ask then, how do you know about it?"

"Back when I was a randy teenager, I found it was a great place where a guy could make out with his girl and not get interrupted. The girl who became my wife says we made our first baby up here."

"Warm memories, huh?"

"The very best."

After some time of rouncing and bouncing and climbing, Bailey stopped the truck. Elaine sensed they were in a flat area although she couldn't be sure with the snow swirling in the headlights and the wind buffeting the truck.

Bailey leaned his forearms on the steering wheel. "We're at the top of the world, young lady from Keats. If it were daylight and clear, you'd see Manhattan over there about four miles—" He gestured toward the passenger window, then swept his hand across to the corner of the windshield on his side of the cab. "—and your town yon way about six miles. Now from here it's all downhill, a splash through Wildcat Creek, up the lane past Charlie Kraft's and scoot on in."

"I can't see a thing. How do you know where we are?"

"I go someplace once," Bailey said, talking with his hands, "every twist and turn of the way is locked in my mind forever. It's God's gift, I guess. . . . Going down."

He let off on the clutch. The truck rolled forward, the nose dropping, the speed picking up, Bailey whipping the steering wheel this way and that, holding on with both hands when the truck bucked over what Elaine could not tell, but the bucking threw her and the clutter off the seat more than a half-dozen times. She heard the splash of water.

A wave washed up into the headlights and over the hood.

Bailey, for the first time, turned on the windshield wipers. They thumped away the water and the snow that plastered itself to the wet glass.

The truck twisted. It rose and whammed down on flat ground.

Bailey flashed a crooked smile in the glow from the panel lights. "We're on Charlie's lane. Easy going until we hit your road and the drifts."

A Farm Bureau membership sign, shaped like a stop sign, loomed up in the lights to the side. Bailey held his speed and spun the steering wheel hard to the left. The tires hammered over something—a dead critter? Elaine wondered—and down onto a smooth run.

Bailey flexed his gloved fingers. "All right, we're on the highway. Here comes the first drift."

Elaine blanched when the world in the headlights went white. A wall of snow washed back over the windshield and the roof of the truck, the wipers thumping away.

Minutes ground on, and more snow drifts, before the wind ceased.

"Keats," Bailey announced. "We're in the trees, protected here, and there's your little place."

He guided the truck off onto a driveway that led down toward Wildcat Creek and a shotgun house, light filtering through the falling snow from the kitchen window. He stopped in the side yard, but before he could get his door open, Elaine was gone— out—running for the back porch. She banged through the kitchen door and into the warmth, the kitchen smelling of fear and disease. Debbie Gibbs, at the table, cradled a girl to herself, the girl half her age and wrapped in a blanket, the girl weeping.

"Mommy, it hurts," the girl said through body-jerking sobs.

"Missus Mars, I got her quiet for a while, got a bit of toast and juice in her, then she went all up."

Elaine took her daughter into her arms. "It's all right, baby, I'm here now. You can stop crying."

"I caaan't. It hurrrts."

"I know. I know." She rocked her. Elaine put her cheek to her daughter's forehead. "You're burning up, child."

Bailey came in from the porch, stamping the snow from his boots. "Fever, huh?"

"I've never felt one so hot, and I've had sick children."

The deputy came to the babysitter. "Debbie, did she throw up?"

"Three times, Mister Devlon."

"Where she hurt?"

"Her stomach. She won't let me touch it."

"Hmm." Bailey swivelled back to Elaine and her daughter. "Mind if I check something?"

"What?"

"Want to see exactly where she hurts. May tell us a thing or two."

"I don't see how."

"Trust me on this."

"All right." To her daughter, Elaine whispered, "Baby, Mister Devlon wants to touch your stomach, is that okay with you?"

"Nooo."

"But he has to, baby."

"Noooooo."

"It's going to be all right. I'm here." Elaine sat down. After she settled her child in her lap, she peeled the blanket back, revealing thin flannel pajamas.

Bailey stripped off his gloves. He knelt before Elaine and her daughter, and eased the pajama top up at the waist. He touched the girl's stomach around the navel.

She howled.

Bailey lifted his fingers away and brought them down again, this time with hardly a feather's touch to the lower left side. "Does it hurt here?"

She whimpered out a no.

"How about here?" Bailey touched the lower right of her stomach.

Tears flowed once more.

"There's swelling here," he said to Elaine. "Stomach's tense as a drum. She have her appendix out?"

"No."

"It's gonna happen now. She's got appendicitis."

"And you know this how?"

"If you need to know, I was a medic in Korea."

"But appendicitis?"

"Hey, I've seen it at least four times, assisted the docs at the aid stations three times with the operations."

"And the fourth time?"

"There wasn't anybody else around, so I had to do it myself. I sure don't want to do that again."

Elaine looked to the babysitter. "Debbie, we've got to go. You stay with my boys, make them breakfast for me."

"I can do that. There's not going to be no school today, snowing like it's been."

"Soon as it gets light, promise me you'll go next door and use the Gilmans' telephone and call your parents. Tell them what's happened, all right? I'll call them, too, when I can."

She did not wait for an answer, instead hefted herself up as she snugged the blanket tight around her daughter. Elaine moved outside with the determination of a locomotive, into the dark and the snow, to the truck. Bailey whipped open the door and half lifted and half shoved the two up and inside. He slammed the door and ran to the other side. Once inside, he backed the truck around and drove out to the county road. He bulled the truck up onto the pavement, shifting up into second gear.

Bailey popped up the switch on his bubble light and grabbed his microphone out of the mess on the seat. He squeezed the transmit button. "Etta Mae, you out there?"

"Your guardian angel as ever is here."

"I've got a girl with appendicitis onboard. Call Doc Walker, wouldja? Tell him to get down to the hospital. We'll be there is fifteen, twenty minutes at the most."

The truck roared out of the protection of the trees at Keats and slammed into a drift. The truck plowed on through.

"Wally on the road?"

"I'm here, Bailey, coming yer way, pushin' the snow. Damn big drifts, I'll tell ya."

"Where are you?"

"Just passed Charlie Krafts'."

"Roger that, keep your grader coming."

The truck banged into another drift. The impact jerked the steering wheel from Bailey's hand and sent the rear into a swing. Elaine in terror crushed her daughter to herself, the girl shrieking.

Bailey chucked the microphone. He scrambled for control of the wheel. When he had it, he cramped the front wheels into the slide, slowed, straightened and stepped down on the gas pedal.

"Sorry 'bout that," he said through rubberband-taut lips, all the time Elaine crooning "Shh shh shh, it's all right, baby, it's all right" to her daughter.

Bailey jutted his jaw to the side, jerked his head and the vertebrae in his neck snapped like popcorn pinging in a hot pan. He kept watch through the windshield, the bubble light's beam arcing around in a ceaseless rhythm, raking through the driving snow. Then he saw it, faint at first and growing stronger with each passing moment, a second bubble light slicing through the snow. Was it moving his way or he toward it? Bailey couldn't be sure. He held to what he hoped was his side of the road, watched the light and then headlights grow and pass to his left, a big yellow grader illuminated by his own headlights.

"Thank you, Wall," he said as he eased the sheriff's truck through a ridge of snow and into the newly cleared lane. He stepped down on the gas.

Perhaps it was the soft, steady rumble of the knobby tires on the pavement that Lanny became quiet, Elaine couldn't be sure, or maybe the girl was just exhausted.

For Bailey, ease returned to his frame as he now steered with one hand. "She's settled down some, huh?"

"Seems to. If you were a medic, didn't you want to be a doctor?"

"Didn't have the patience for all those years of college. And when I got home, the sheriff was hiring and I needed a job and it seemed like a good fit. Besides, he was my uncle."

"Family sure helps."

"How about yours?"

"My daddy's a merchant marine. I see him every couple years."

"And your mom?"

"I guess she got tired of waiting for Daddy to come home. Short time after I got married, she just packed the car and left. I don't know where she is."

Bailey nodded at the windshield. "Look up ahead there. First lights of Manhattan—Ernie's Mobile station. He stays open all night. 'Course it helps that he lives just the next street over. . . . Your girl still all right?"

Elaine put her hand on her daughter's forehead. "Fever's not changed."

"Well, we're only a couple blocks from the hospital now." Bailey shifted down. He cranked the steering wheel to the left and bulled the truck into what appeared in the headlights to be an unplowed street. Bailey held tight to the steering wheel as the tires chewed on. "Oh-oh."

Elaine glanced across the cab.

"Car cattywumpus in the street," Bailey said. "Musta spun out. You ready for a little front-yard driving?"

"What's that?"

The deputy shifted down one more time. He herded the truck up and over a curb, across a sidewalk, missed a shagbark hickory, and romped over a cluster of bushes poking through the snow.

Bailey drove back out into the street. "I'm gonna catch hell for this. That was Doc Walker's place. Those rose bushes, he's kinda proud of them."

At the end of the street he drove under a light that illuminated the front door of Memorial Hospital, the snow there filtering down rather than whipping horizontal. He stopped and hustled Elaine and her daughter out of the truck and up the steps. They kicked their way inside to where a man in an overcoat, his pajama top showing through the open throat, stood visiting with a woman in white. Both turned toward the new arrivals.

The man peered over top of glasses that rode low on the bridge of his nose. "Bailey, you get me out at the damnedest times. This as serious as Etta Mae said?"

"Have I ever been wrong?" Bailey pushed Elaine forward, her daughter stirring in her arms. "Doc, this is Elaine Mars and her girl, Lanny. It all musta gone bad around midnight and, well, you check her over."

Walker leaned in. "How you doing, little one?"

The girl winced. "My stomach."

"Yes, well, I want to touch your forehead, is that all right?"

Lanny gave the slightest nod.

Walker put the palm of his hand on her forehead. "Tad warm there, isn't it? I understand you threw up a couple times."

She scrunched her face.

"Yes, it isn't any fun. Now I'm going to touch your stomach like old Deputy Bailey did." Walker slipped his hand beneath the blanket, to under Lanny's pajama top.

She cried.

"Shh-shh-shh, that's all right." He looked up over his glasses to Elaine, his forehead furrowing. "I hate to tell you, Bailey's right."

"SO YOU'RE gonna get her home tomorrow, huh, for Christmas?" Eddie Wilson asked, a foot resting on a chair, his arms folded across his knee. J.D. Castro stood beside him, leaning on Wilson's shoulder.

Elaine, seated and with a half-eaten porkchop in front of her, wiped at the exhaustion on her face. "That's what Doctor Walker says. Having Lanny back, that's going to be our Christmas and nothing more now that I've got a hospital bill to pay."

"There's always Santy Claus," Castro said.

"J.D., I found out at age ten that Mom and Dad were Santa Claus, and they're gone."

"Well, you never know."

Wilson elbowed his driving partner who choked on his tongue, while Elaine focused her effort on cutting a bite from her porkchop. "I guess I'm just lucky that Gracie keeps running and we've got food and heat. We wouldn't have that if it weren't for washing dishes here."

The bell over the door jingled.

Bailey Devlon rambled in, kicking snow from his boots. He called out, "Elaine, you rob all the stores in town?"

She stopped, her fork midway to her mouth. "Pardon?"

"Your car. It's jammed with stuff."

"There's nothing in my car."

"Hey, I know what nothing looks like, and there are sacks of groceries in the front seat and boxes of what all I don't know in the back."

"Can't be."

Eddie turned away from Elaine. He did a wave-off to Bailey, but Bailey only arched an eyebrow. "Go look for yourself."

She rose. She hustled away from the table and on outside, not pausing to grab her mackinaw. Bailey came along. He aimed his flashlight at Gracie.

Elaine sucked in a lungful of crystalline cold air as she peered through the side window. "This can't be."

She opened the back door and ran her hand up to the top of the carton nearest her, large enough that it could hold a dorm room-sized refrigerator. Elaine opened the carton. She reached in and brought out a pair of blue jeans. "A whole box of pants. Kids' sizes it says here."

She pawed her way into another carton. "Shoes. I'd guess a dozen pair. And there's a box that says shirts."

Bailey opened the opposite door. He reached into a bag. When his hand came out, it held a Tonka truck. Bailey brought it up to the dome light. "I'd say you've got a raft of toys in these other bags."

Elaine came around. She opened the front passenger door and poked into the sacks she found there. "A frozen turkey, and it looks like all the makings for a dinner and more. Did you do this?"

"Hey, I just got here."

Elaine glanced up through the windshield, to the front window of Bernie's. There stood Wilson, Castro, and Tibby Watson together, staring back. "Did they?"

"I wouldn't know. My job is to investigate thefts, not gifts."

"Well, somebody did this."

"How about we chalk it up to Santa Claus?"

"J.D.," Elaine said.

"Aw, he's hardly got two nickels to rub together, and when he's got two, he drops one in the pinball machine."

Elaine slammed the car door. She stalked back to the diner with Bailey hustling after her. Inside she found no one at the window, all instead sitting around Robert-the-cook's table in the back corner, each holding a hand of cards.

Wilson threw two down. "Gimme a couple fresh ones, Tib."

She shot two replacements his way.

Elaine marched up. She planted her hands, fingers spread wide, in the middle of the table. "All right, I want to know who did this."

Tibby winged three cards to Castro waggling three fingers at her. "Did what?"

"Put all that stuff in my car—jeans, toys, a turkey."

"Maybe Santa Claus, who you don't believe in, has some helpers."

"You did it, all of you."

Tibby laughed. She threw down her hand and dealt herself a new set of cards.

Robert-the-cook, staring at his hand, popped a raisin into his mouth. "Oh, I'm supposed to tell you from Bernie, you're to take the rest of the darned night off. I don't know why, something about presents you gotta wrap."

"I don't have any wrapping paper."

Castro scraped his cards against his whisker-shadowed chin, working at an itch. "You look on the floor in the backseat?"

Note: Beth Henley's 1979 play *Crimes of the Heart* is the inspiration for this story. The three sisters in Henley's play, raised in a dysfunctional family, have to work through a host of personal problems when they come back together after one shoots her abusive husband. It's a tragic play at times and at times hilariously funny. The play won a Pulitzer Prize for Drama. I got to wondering, what if it were four sisters and three of them were gathering for a Christmas season family ritual . . . baking cookies together?

The Fourth Sister

A GREAT stamping of boots came from the kitchen porch, yet Shar Wextral did not turn away from her work. Instead, she poured more energy into stirring the filling for her lemon tea cookies, the filling bubbling in a saucepan on the stove. "That's gotta be Marileth," she muttered. "Let her in, wouldja, Rose?"

Rose—Rosella Baker—making thumbprints in balls of cookie dough, wiped her hands on her apron as she hurried to the back door.

Shartre Wextral, Rosella Baker, Marileth Dobbs—the Stackpole girls long married, three peas in a pod their dad liked to call them when they were little, a year apart in ages with Shar the oldest and for some ten years the titular head of the family as a consequence of their parents' death in a car accident not two miles from home.

There had been a fourth—Jonna—but, as Shar told her children when they asked after their aunt, she had wandered off the reservation. Wandered off and just as well. A bad penny good to be rid of, but this last part she only said to her sisters.

"Sorry to be late," Marileth said out of breath when the door opened for her, her hair frazzled, that which could be seen sticking out from beneath her scarf. "A little company at the house."

"Who?" Rose asked.

Marileth bustled into the warmth in which the aromas of vanilla and cinnamon mingled themselves with ginger, a Food Lion grocery bag clutched in one arm and in her free hand a basket. She dumped both on kitchen chairs before she leaned against the wall to pull off her snow boots. "First year in what, five has it been, that we're going to have a white Christmas?"

Rose closed the storm and the inside doors. "Who's your company, Sis?"

"Later. Right now I've gotta hurry to catch up with you two. You're probably way ahead of me."

Shar, her graying hair permed and frosted special for the holidays, arched an eyebrow. "If you'd get up in the morning."

"Just because your Duane has forgotten what sex is anymore doesn't mean my Charlie has." Marileth tossed a boot toward the warm-air register.

Shar dipped a finger into the lemony filling, to taste it. "Don't you start in on Duane."

"But it's true."

"I know it's true, but don't start in on him anyway." She put her fingertip into her mouth.

The stove timer went off, startling Rosella, the slender one of the three—the nervous one. She whipped open the oven door and, with her apron as a hot pad, pulled out a sheet of butter cookies, each with a thumbprint in the center. She set the sheet on a cooling rack and whisked the pan of cookies she'd been preparing into the oven.

Shar shook her mixing spoon at the late comer. "I've got five kids, well, four. That's enough, thank you."

Marileth, auburn hair and, unlike her sisters, not a strand of gray showing, tossed her second boot toward the register. It hit down hard, slapping the other boot onto its side. "There is this little pill, you know."

"Don't believe in it."

"You're a Catholic now?"

"Don't believe in that, either." Shar carried her saucepan to the cooling rack. There she turned a half-teaspoon of filling into the first thumbprint. "Rose, get the coconut from the cupboard. Come sprinkle some on." She filled more thumbprints. "Mare, Primitive Baptist was good enough for Momma, so it's good enough for me, and it oughtta be good enough for you."

"I suppose." Marileth stripped off her cloth coat and scarf. She stuffed the scarf in a pocket while she peered about for a chair to lay her coat over.

"Closet," Shar said, giving her sister a cold look as she spooned the lemon filling into the depressions on the remaining cookies.

Rose moved in beside her older sister. She scattered coconut shreds over the filling. "You know you could use powdered sugar. Always have in the past."

"This year I want something different. You about ready to roll out your gingerbread?"

"I'd better get at it. Five, six minutes and the oven will be free."

Marileth, out of her coat, emptied the Food Lion bag onto a side counter, ingredients for mini-fruitcakes. From her basket, she brought out a brown crockery mixing bowl that had been her mother's and her grandmother's before.

"By rights," Shar said as she cast a lustful look at the bowl, "that should be mine."

"I'll be sure to put it in my will."

"My God, I'll be eighty-six before you die."

Marileth laughed at that. "Naw, ninety-three. We Stackpoles live a looong time."

Rose spread a handful of flour over the table, then dumped the gingerbread dough from her mixing bowl onto the flour. She brought out her marble rolling pin and rolled the mass into a thin layer, pushing the rolling pin first one way, then pulling it the other.

Shar glanced at the container of candied fruit in Marileth's hand. "Funny makings for sugar cookies."

"That's because I'm not making sugar cookies."

The smile slipped from Rose's face. "No?"

"Saw this recipe in the paper and I thought, like Shar, why not something different?" Marileth poured molasses into a saucepan before she added a quarter-cup of water and a splash of vanilla. "These are gonna be the neatest little fruitcakes. You bake them in miniature muffin tins like this." She held up a tin from her basket.

"But we've always had your sugar cookies, used our cookie cutters to make wreaths and stars and snowmen, and we've decorated them. It's Christmas, Marileth. It's a tradition."

"Time for a new tradition." She poured a box of golden raisins into the mixture and put the saucepan on a burner.

"Well, if they turn out like Momma's fruitcake," Shar said, "Duane can use them for skeet shooting, instead of clay pigeons."

"Oh, you are so funny." Marileth turned to the table. She pinched a piece of the gingerbread dough and popped it in her mouth. She mulled over the taste. "You didn't use molasses."

Rose pushed the rolling pin forward over the dough circle. "I never use molasses. I always use sorghum. You know we grow our own cane. Tommy crushes it every year and boils the juice down. Why do you always ask if I'm using molasses?"

Marileth squeezed her sister's shoulder. "I like molasses in my gingerbread."

"Then you make it. I notice you never complain when you eat my gingerbread men."

Shar opened one of her utensil drawers. She sorted through until she found the gingerbread man cutter. This she passed to Rose. "Marileth never complains about anything that goes in her mouth. Got the wide hips to prove it, right, Sis?"

"Charlie likes me plump."

"Uh-huhh."

Marileth peered into her grocery bag, next her basket. "Ooo, I forgot the butter."

"Plenty on the table."

"Thanks. I owe you."

"Just leave Momma's mixing bowl and I'll forgive the debt."

That caused Marileth to pause, but when she heard Shar chortling, she, too, laughed. Marileth helped herself to the butter box. From it, she took two sticks, peeled off the wrappings, and squished the butter in her crockery bowl with the back of her mixing spoon. "Just so you don't worry needlessly, I have someone else making the sugar cookies."

"And who would that be?" Shar asked as she went back to her work of lifting the finished tea cookies from the baking sheet onto a plate. When she had that done, she greased the sheet and set it on the table where Rose cut out one gingerbread man after another. "Sis, would you put the men on the sheet for me? And, Marileth, who's making the sugar cookies? Are we going to bake and decorate them here?"

Marileth added two-thirds of a cup of sugar to the butter. "The who, you'll see. The baking and decorating, yes, we'll do it here."

Rose nudged Shar. "I get it. Denise is twelve now. Mommy has her doing the sugar cookies for a Four-H project."

Marileth cracked an egg. She let the yolk and white slip from its shell into the butter and sugar. "Could be."

"Certainly is mysterious."

Marileth stirred in the egg. "You two old fuds need a little mystery in your lives."

"I'm only a year older than you, and Shar, just two."

"Uh-huh." She cracked a second egg into her mixing bowl. "Shar, you doing all right?"

"Of course." The older sister slipped another gingerbread man onto the cookie sheet.

"I mean it's only been a week since we buried Ricky. You have reason to be upset. You know we don't have to be making cookies."

Rose gathered the gingerbread scraps into a dough ball. "It's therapy."

Shar wiped the back of her hand at the corner of her eye. "It's not therapy. Baking cookies is, well, it's what we do at Christmas."

"Mm-hmm."

"Look, I've never bought Christmas cookies at the Food Lion, and I'm not starting now." She picked up the next gingerbread man, turned it, and slipped it onto the cookie sheet.

"Still and all—"

"Mare, I'm all cried out. I'm not angry anymore. It was an accident, and there's nothing I can do about it."

The oven timer interrupted. Rose hurried over and took out a pan of tea cookies. As she stepped to the side, Shar slid her sheet of gingerbread men into the oven and turned the temperature knob up a notch.

"So who was your company?" Rose again asked her younger sister, shifting the conversation away from the death of Shar's seventeen-year-old, her last child, her pride, a handsome youth with the square face and ruddy good looks that had drawn her to Duane Wextral, the man who would become her husband, who fathered the boy.

In a second mixing bowl, Marileth dumped flour, baking soda, cinnamon, nutmeg, allspice, and cloves. She stirred away. "This is going to be so good."

Rose slapped her ball of gingerbread down on the table. "You're not answering my question."

"I'm not. You want me to make up the frosting for you? I'm at a breakpoint here."

"I'd appreciate it. Now to your company."

Marileth lifted a box of powdered sugar from her grocery bag. She measured the first of two cups into a mixing bowl. "Patience," she said.

"Oh, you're going to have your company drop by and help us."

"You finally figured it out."

"So I take it we know this company."

"Uh-huh." To the powdered sugar Marileth added water. She stirred, working the two into a smooth frosting.

"But you're not going to tell us?"

"Like all good Christmas gifts, company should be a surprise."

Shar finished filling the last thumbprint of her pan of tea cookies and set the saucepan in the sink. "I've had enough of surprises—Tony-the-cop coming to the door."

"It's not that," Marileth said. She split half the frosting into a second bowl, then rummaged in her grocery bag for the food colorings. "You want white and what else?"

Rose set her rolling pin aside and picked up the cutter. "Surprise me."

"Blue."

"No, not blue."

"Red?"

"I've always used red."

"Green?"

"I think not."

"I thought I was supposed to pick the color."

"You are."

"Then it's gonna be orange."

During this color conversation, Shar set her tea cookies onto a second plate. That done, she greased the pan for the gingerbread men and lifted the men from the flour-covered table onto the pan.

Once more the oven timer went off. Rose wrapped her apron around her hand and took the hot cookie sheet with its fresh-baked gingerbread men from the oven to a rack on the counter. A knock rattled the kitchen door as Rose moved across the kitchen. "I'll get it," she sang out.

Shar picked up the cookie pan and turned toward the oven as Rose, having opened the back door, stood there, her face a portrait of shock.

Shar glanced her way. The pan slipped from her hand. It clattered on the linoleum, the gingerbread men jumbling themselves, several flipping out of the pan. "No. No! I'll not have her in my house."

The woman in the doorway, her face thin and drawn, took a tighter hold on the covered bowl she carried. Her smile, what little there was, fled, replaced by pain. "I knew this wasn't going to work," she said. She, Jonna Stackpole Harden.

Marileth hurried over. She reached past Rose frozen to the floor, her mouth open, and caught Jonna by the elbow. "You don't back out now. Remember why you came here."

"But—"

"Remember, you've got peace to make."

Shar reached for the rolling pin on the table. "Not with me she won't."

Marileth squared around to her older sister. "It's been sixteen years for God's sake."

"I don't care if it's been a hundred and sixteen years. She had sex with my husband, and I caught them at it."

"It was wrong, we all know it, but Jonna's husband had just walked out on her. She was hurt, Shar. She was vulnerable, and Duane had dated Jonna before he ever took up with you. Have you forgotten that?"

"That may justify it in your eyes, but it don't work for me."

"It's past, Shar. It can't be changed." Marileth put a hand on her oldest sister's arm. "You don't know how hard it's been for Jonna to come home after all these years. I do. We've cried together for the last two days."

Shar turned away, to put her kitchen table between herself and the interloper, this kid sister, this sinner. "I don't have to listen to this."

"Oh yes, you do." Marileth took a picture from her pocket. She pressed it into Shar's hand white with flour.

Shar glanced at the photo. "This is my Ricky. When did you take this?"

"I didn't."

"I don't understand."

"Jonna took it."

"But she—"

"Sixteen years she's lived in Oregon now."

"Then she couldn't."

"That's right. She couldn't. It isn't Ricky."

"Then who?"

"It's Jonna's son, your nephew."

"But look at his face."

"I know. Just like Ricky's. Just like Duane's. This is Duane's son."

"Bastard."

"Yes. That's right." Marileth pushed Shar toward a chair. "And like Ricky, the boy's dead."

The anger that had flamed around Shar's eyes gave way to confusion, then grief. She eased herself down.

Marileth stood beside her. "Darrell was fifteen. He got angry one evening with his mother—with Jonna, yes—and stole her car."

"No."

"He did. He was speeding, the police told Jonna, when they lit out after him. Five miles they chased him, and then Darrell lost control."

Shar began to wail, tears slipping from her eyes.

"Jonna says you need to know it all," Marileth said.

"I don't want to."

"Shar, the car rolled over twice. It hit a tree and the gas tank exploded. Jonna's boy, he burned to death because no one could get close enough to the car to save him. Shar, he was half-brother to Ricky."

"Did—did she know about Ricky?"

Jonna, also in tears, inched up to the table. She sat down across from her oldest sister. "I'm sorry for you. I didn't know until I came home, to Marileth's."

Shar took a handkerchief from her apron pocket. She waved a hand at Jonna, as if that might make her disappear. She turned away, covering her tears.

Marileth gazed at Jonna. She gestured toward Shar.

The fourth sister, with an effort, forced herself to choke back her tears. She pushed off from her chair and came around to Shar. She knelt before her. "I'm sorry."

"You want me to say I forgive you?"

"No. I just want you to know I'm sorry. I'm sorry for everything, for Duane, for Ricky, for everything."

"And that's supposed to make it all better?"

Marileth stepped behind her oldest sister. She put her hands on Shar's trembling shoulders, quavering from emotions too long held captive. Marileth leaned down. "Jonna has nothing now. Her family was her son."

Shar wiped at her nose. "When?"

Jonna knit the fingers of her hands together. "Six months ago."

"And you're just coming back now to tell us?"

"Shar," Marileth said, "she drank herself into forgetfulness before the funeral of her boy. She was found wandering, and a judge ordered her into rehab. She was only released last week."

"That don't cut no grass with me."

"Jonna came out to find that the bank had foreclosed on her house, her job gone. All she had was the clothes in her suitcase and eighty-five dollars she hadn't drunk up, hardly enough for a bus ticket."

Shar glanced up at Marileth. "So she came to you?"

"She knew she couldn't come to you, not right off. . . . She wants to make peace. This is the season for it."

The oldest sister covered her eyes with her handkerchief. "God, this is hard."

"I know."

"You can't. You haven't lost a son."

"But Jonna has."

Shar lowered her handkerchief, revealing eyes swimming in grief. She glanced to the side, toward Jonna.

Jonna's hand came up.

Shar with reluctance took it. She felt that hand, a hand she had not known for sixteen years. She felt it squeeze her hand. She could not help herself, she squeezed the hand in return.

Shar pulled Jonna to her.

They embraced, sobs filling the spaces where words could not be.

Marileth touched at the tear in the corner of her own eye. She turned away, but was alone for only a moment. Rose came to her, the gingerbread man cutter in her hand. She put an arm around her sister's shoulders. "Sis, this sure is one Christmas for the books."

Note: A writing prompt launched "Reunion" . . . the prompt: It was the best Christmas ever, or maybe it was the worst Christmas ever. Write a 300-word story, said the directions. I chose best because this was to be a James Early Christmas. Five drafts and I brought the story in at 311 words. I just could not squeeze out those last 11. But like every good story that gets a strong set of legs under it, I knew this one did not end where the rule forced me to end it. One more bit of information. The year is 1948 which makes this story a prequel to *Early's Fall*. Early, at this moment, has been the sheriff of Riley County for less than a year.

Reunion with Molly

JAMES EARLY stood at the roadside, hunched up and hopping from one foot to the other to keep warm, hoping he wouldn't turn into a popsicle before his ride came.

A horn sounded.

Early, still hopping, turned in its direction.

A Hudson Commodore Six came around a bend in the county road. The car, a four-door, glided into the opposing traffic lane—no traffic on so cold a day—and stopped beside Early.

The driver, county clerk Clovis Henthorn, cranked down his window. "Hey, sheriff, hope we didn't keep you waitin' too long. When you've got a brood of kids like ours to get ready—" He gazed at the pile of gear on the ground next to Early. "Wanna stow yer stuff in the trunk?"

"It's that or tie it on the roof."

Henthorn horsed himself out and opened the trunk. When he stepped aside, Early pitched in a saddle, saddle blanket, and a collection of odds and ends, including a bridle, his chaps and a duster. He shifted them around to avoid crushing a bulky sack in the back corner of the trunk, the sack showing Christmas wrapping from the top, and a hamper that Early figured was packed with diapers and clothes for the Henthorns' baby up in the front seat in her mother's arms.

Henthorn opened a back passenger door. He stuck his head in. "You young'uns, squish over there so Mister Early can get in. Like I told you, he's ridin' with us a ways. Any complaining, he's the sheriff. He'll put you in the pokey."

Four children jostled themselves toward the far door.

Early wedged in. He touched the shoulder of the closest. "Maybe it'd make more room if you sat on my lap."

The child—a girl—clambered around and, with Early's help, resettled herself on his lap. "Yer kinda cold, Mister," she said.

"Well, I've been outside for a bit. If your dad's heater's working, I'll warm up."

Henthorn got back in behind the steering wheel and slammed the door. After he got the car rolling, he glanced up at Early's image in the corner of his mirror. "Sheriff, that's Mary on yer lap. She's four and a tad small for her age. Next to you, we got Mark, Luke, and John—nine, ten, and eleven. They're our stair-step babies from before the war. Up front here with Ruthie is our youngest, Naomi. She's not nine months yet. And the last here between us, our squirmy little guy, this is Seth."

Early brushed a finger across the tip of his nose. "Bible names."

"Yup, Ruthie insisted. That's the tradition in her family."

Ruth Henthorn laughed and hugged her baby. "Mister Early, Clovis is not big on names. After our third, he said we just oughtta number our children and be done with it."

Henthorn leaned back, steering with his left hand, his right arm draped around his youngest boy. "Yup, that's true. I did."

Mary looked up at Early. "You comin' to Grampa an' Gramma's ranch with us?"

Early shook his head. "That's be nice, but your dad's gonna drop me off outside of Council Grove."

"Why?"

"Did you see the saddle I put in the trunk?"

"Uh-huh."

"I'm gonna see a rancher about getting a horse for Christmas."

She grinned. "Can we see him?"

"Him is a her. Maybe I can arrange it when we get her home."

"I'd like that. Pa won't let us have a horse."

Henthorn shot a look up at the mirror. "Baby, we live in town."

Mark, the oldest, at the far side of the backseat, leaned forward. He gazed at Early. "Sheriff, do you have a gun?"

"Not with me."

"Oh."

"Does that disappoint you?"

"I've asked Pa for a twenty-two."

"What'd he say?"

"I'm not old enough."

"You're eleven, right?"

"Uh-huh."

"When I was eleven, my dad started me out with a Daisy, you know, an air rifle."

"A B-B gun?"

"I got real accurate with it. I was fifteen before my dad gave me a twenty-two."

Henthorn looked up at Early in the mirror and waved an okay sign.

HENTHORN, rolling east out of Council Grove, slowed for the turnoff onto a ranch lane. "This it, Jimmy?" he asked, glancing up in the mirror.

"The Lazy K, yup. You can let me out here. I can walk in."

"With that load, won't hear of it." Henthorn wheeled his Hudson off the highway scraped clean onto a track in the snow made by a vehicle with dual rear wheels. "Somebody's busted a trail for us, how about that."

He shifted down to second and ground on, the motor whining. "Jimmy, how long you figure it'll take to ride your horse home?"

"Should make it sometime after dark."

"It's gonna be damn cold out there."

"I got my long johns on."

Henthorn herded the car through a gate left open and into the yard of a ranchstead. There he swung the car around and up to the house, smoke drifting up from the house's chimney.

Early squeezed the shoulder of the little girl asleep on his lap. "Mary, this is where I get out."

She lifted her eye lids and yawned.

He pushed the door open. As he slid out, he set the girl back on the seat next to her brother John. She snuggled in under his arm and again closed her eyes.

Early eased the door shut. He went back to the trunk already open and grabbed his saddle and half his gear and set it out on the porch.

Henthorn brought the rest. "Go peck on the door. I'll wait here 'til I'm sure yer in good order."

Early sucked in a deep breath. He brushed his gloved hands on his jeans, then clomped up the steps to the door. There he rapped and waited.

After some moments, the door opened.

Early found himself staring into the face of a man his father's age, the man half leaning against the jamb. "Mister Krem?" he asked.

"That be me. You Mister Early?"

"Yessir."

Krem straightened himself up. "Looks like you've grown a mustache since I saw you last back at your ranch sale."

"Yup. The mustache keeps my upper lip from freezing on days like this." Early wiped the back of his gloved hand across his cookie duster. He sniffed at the air. "Smells like Christmas in your house."

"Yeah, the wife's baking cinnamon rolls. The grandkids like them."

"I'll bet." Early shifted his weight, suggesting a change in the conversation. "Like I said on the phone, I've got a job now, sheriff of Riley County. Pay's good, so I've come to buy back my horse."

Krem reached inside the jamb for his hat and mackinaw. After he togged himself up, he came out on the porch, closing the door behind him. "You got a truck or a horse trailer?"

Early tilted his head toward his pile of gear.

Krem stared at it. "You intend to ride her to Manhattan? Lordy, Mister Early, there's a blizzard on the way."

"By the radio weather report, I'm thinking I ought to be able to make it before it hits."

"Hope yer right."

"Anyway, I figure the long ride is the best way for Molly and me to get reacquainted."

Henthorn cleared his throat. When Early glanced his way, Henthorn waved goodbye and plodded around to the driver's side of the car. He got in and drove off.

Early and Krem watched the car recede into the distance. Finally, Krem stepped down from the porch. "Appears you brought everything except the feed trough," he said as he gathered up all the loose stuff.

Early, on the ground, too, hefted the saddle and saddle blanket up on his shoulder. He steadied the load by holding onto the saddle horn. The bridle, Early scooped up with his free hand and hurried after Krem already kicking through the snow toward a low-slung barn, the siding bleached a silvery gray by hard years of sun. "You mentioned a feed trough," Early said when he caught up. "I've got a feed bag and some grain in one of my saddle bags. Long ride, I expect I'm gonna have to refuel Molly at some point."

"You pack some food for yerself?"

"No sir, it'd freeze. I had myself an extra-large breakfast that ought to carry me the day."

Krem opened the barn door enough that he and Early could squeeze through, then closed it quick before the warmth from his livestock could escape.

Early inhaled the smells of horses and dry prairie hay. He grinned.

"Right this way, Mister Early." Krem led the way to a stall about midway in the barn.

A brown mare, her winter coat thick and fluffed out, leaned her head over the half door. She whiffled and bobbed her head.

Krem rubbed her face. "Old girl, the boss man's here. You're goin' home."

He stepped aside, and Early moved in. The horse whiffled again and shoved her muzzle under Early's arm, jostling him. He stroked the side of her face. "Molly, I've missed you a heap."

"Mister Early, it's pretty obvious she's missed you, too."

"How much?" Early asked.

"How much for your horse? I paid seventy-five at the auction."

"How much do you want?"

Krem rubbed at a sideburn. "Well, the wife and I've talked about that. I know how much my horses mean to me. If I had to sell one or the mess of them, I'd sure want them back. Mister Early, Molly's yours."

"Seventy-five then?"

"No, Mister Early, she's yours. A gift. It's Christmas."

Early twisted around. Before he could say something, Molly butted him in the small of his back.

Krem chuckled. "I think she wants to get goin'."

"I don't know what to say, other than thank you."

"You don't even have to say that."

A crooked grin poked up at the corner of Early's mustache. He turned around to Molly, slipped the bridle over her head, and led her out into the alley. There he tacked her up—saddle blanket, saddle, a lariat tied to the pommel, saddle bags behind the seat, a canvas roll laying across the bags, tied there to keep it secure.

Krem lifted one of Molly's front hooves onto his knee. "Put new shoes on her a couple weeks ago." He wiggled the iron shoe. "Still tight. I checked them all this morning, so she's ready to travel."

Early strapped on his chaps and shrugged his duster on over his sheepskin coat. After he snugged his hands into gloves—wool-lined—he led Molly outside and swung up into the saddle. She danced. Early reined her in, kneeing her around to Krem.

"I get WIBW down here," Krem said. "Last I heard, the blizzard's in Salina. If it catches you, you look for a place to tuck in."

"I'll do that."

Krem reached up, and Early clapped onto the rancher's hand, gave it a firm shake. "I do thank you, I really do, for taking care of Mol."

"She's earned her keep. Mister Early, maybe the wife an' I'll come up an' see you sometime this summer."

"You do that, Mister Krem. We'll show you a good time." Early turned Molly toward the lane, and she leaped out in an instant gallop, her hooves pitching up snow as she pounded away toward the highway.

EARLY SLOW WALKED Molly into Council Grove. As they neared a café, he smelled wood smoke and baking ham. He knew he needed to make tracks, but the thought of a hot ham sandwich . . . Early stepped down from Molly. He tied her to a light pole in front of the café and went on inside. Music greeted him from a radio over the pass-thru, an organ and choir, the choir singing 'It Came upon a Midnight Clear.'

Early stripped off his gloves and settled on a stool at the counter.

A man, with an apron tied up under his arms, came out from the kitchen. "Howdy, stranger," he said as he polished his hands on his apron. "What kin I do ya fer?"

"How about a hot ham sandwich to go and a slurp of coffee while I wait for it? I've gotta keep riding."

The cook brought up a porcelain cup from beneath the counter and filled it from a pot simmering on a hotplate. "Ridin', like on a horse? Man, it's damn cold out there."

Early picked up the cup. He cradled it in his hands, the cup's warmth welcome. "With this and a hot sandwich, I'll be fine," Early said. "Make it with that extra thick Texas bread, wouldja?"

The cook shambled back into the kitchen, leaving Early to sip at his coffee. The heat from it felt good in his belly. He pitched up his voice to be heard across the swinging door. "You got any cookies I can take with me?"

"Chocolate chip an' oatmeal raisin. Fresh baked this mornin'."

"Put a couple handfuls in a paper poke for me, wouldja?"

"You got it, mister. Where you bound fer?"

"Manhattan." Early again sipped at his coffee. He heard the crinkle of waxed paper being folded.

"That's thirty-five mile," came the cook's voice from the kitchen.

"If Mol and I make good time, we ought to be there and in the barn by nightfall."

"Yer gonna be in snow, ya know that."

"That's what people keep telling me."

"Could be bad snow. We went overcast about an hour ago."

"I know. The wind's picking up."

The cook shambled back in carrying a paper sack. He planted it on the counter in front of Early.

"How much?"

"Nuthin'. It's on the house."

Early arched an eyebrow.

The cook flicked a thumb across a crease in the top of the bag. "Hey, man, it's Christmas. Well, almost. I'm feelin' a mite charitable."

Early pushed off the stool with his sack. "Thank you. By the way, your coffee's right good."

"Glad you liked it." He wriggled his fingers at the sack. "I put yer sammich on top so you kin get at it easy."

Early, back in his gloves at the door, waved his appreciation.

The cook jutted his chin up. "You have a good Christmas tomorrow, mister."

"You, too."

Early departed to the sounds of the choir on the radio singing 'God Rest Ye Merry Gentlemen.' He hummed the tune as he untied Molly's reins and stepped up into the saddle. She snorted at the first snowflakes drifting down and stepped out for the road going north.

THREE HIOURS ON, Early rode hunched down, a muffler over his hat and tied under his chin, to keep his hat from blowing away. Snow pelted the side of his face. Molly, her head hanging low, flicked her left ear at the snow attempting to burrow inside. From time to time, she snorted, blasting her nostrils clear.

Early squinted off to the side, at a mound in the field that paralleled the highway, the mound some twenty yards away. Likely a hay stack, he thought, and turned Molly off the road. She plunged down into the ditch, snow up over her knees. At the line fence, Early stepped off. He pushed the top barbed wire down and clicked his tongue, encouraging Molly forward. With the wind whistling up her butt, she stepped gingerly over the wire.

Early followed. He grabbed Molly's reins and took off on a run, his chaps slapping, she trotting behind him. He led her around to the lee side of the haystack. There Early hauled hay down and spread it deep for a makeshift bed for Molly and himself. When he had it ready, he pushed her around against the stack and lifted her saddle away. Early, clicking his tongue again, tugged down on Molly's reins. She knelt and rocked back, her legs tucking beneath her.

Early shook out his canvas roll and draped it over Molly. From a saddle bag, he brought out a feed bag made of stiff canvas, the bag half full with oats. He pushed it into the hay in front of Molly.

She snuffled into it.

For himself, Early crawled under the canvas. In the new dark, he leaned his back against Molly and took a cookie from his poke, a chocolate chip by the feel of the knobs on it. He ate and listened to the roar of the wind coming over the top of the haystack, listened to the stir and swirl of snow packing down on the canvas. "Girl," he said, fingering what was left of his cookie, "looks like we're gonna be here a while."

EARLY WOKE to silence.

He poked up the near edge of the canvas and peered out at a world of white dazzled by a nearly full moon. Storm's passed, yeah. Wonder when?

Early prodded with two fingers into his watch pocket, but nothing. Wonder what else I forgot?

He clambered out, pushed himself up on his feet, and stamped around, to get feeling back into them. Early swept his gloved hands down the sides of his duster, brushing away strands of prairie hay stuck to the fabric. When done, he lifted the canvas and the drift of snow on top of it away from Molly.

She whiffled, pleased, he thought, to be in the open air again. Up came her rear and she stood and shook herself, arching her back and wringing her tail.

Early snapped the canvas, sending the snow that had covered it flying. He snapped the canvas a second time. When he had it clean, he rolled it up, tacked up Molly, and tied the canvas on top of the saddlebags.

Ready, Early climbed aboard.

Molly stepped out, her breath steaming in the crisp night air. She kicked through the drift on the lee side until clear of the stack where Early guided her to the west, back toward the road. At the fence, they drifted north, Molly plodding on until they came on a gate. Early stepped down. He opened the gate, led Molly through, closed the gate and rode on, on the graveled state highway in places deeply drifted, in others the snow blown clear.

Early grubbed out a cookie from his poke, an oatmeal raisin by the feel of it.

He bit down . . . and spit out a fragment.

Frozen.

A tooth breaker.

Early reached the cookie forward to Molly, and she took it from his gloved hand.

"At least one of us gets to enjoy it," he murmured.

Some further on, something odd broke Early out of his funk, something ahead, out of place, a car in the ditch, the side a solid white. The closer he and Molly came, the more clearly he heard it . . . the car's motor burbling.

"What in heaven's—"

He stepped down. He waded into the ditch and rubbed the snow away from the driver's window glass.

The window rolled down.

Early peered in at a man slouched behind the steering wheel. "What happened here?" Early asked.

The man stared back. "Whaddaya think?"

"Looks like you're stuck in the ditch."

"Got that right, fella."

"If you don't mind me asking, whatcha doing out here?"

The man braced his hands against the top of the steering wheel. "Waiting for someone like you to come by and ask a damn-fool question. Look, I slid off the road on my way to the W-Bar-N. This is as far as I got."

"And?"

He threw up a hand. "And I wasn't gonna walk from here and freeze to death."

"Yup. Guess I wouldn't, either."

"Look, you got a chain and a tow or should I zip up the glass to keep warm 'til somebody else comes along? I'm not outta gas yet."

Early leaned an elbow against the top of the door frame. "Well, all I've got is my horse. I could give you a ride. How far's this ranch?"

The man switched off the car's motor. "A couple miles. The buildings are off to the west in a little canyon." He forced himself out and into the snow, the snow filling his unbuckled three-bucklers. He reached back in for something and held it up for Early to see—a black bag.

"You're a doc?"

"Very observant. One of the sisters at the ranch has a broke ankle."

"So that's why you're out here."

"Got that right."

"Then we better get you on. Doc, I'm James Early."

"Mister Early, you can call me Goody, Goody Divine. I doctor back in the Grove." Divine, in his overcoat, thrust his hands into heavy gloves and slapped an earlapper cap on his head. "Appreciate the ride."

"Least I can do."

Divine slogged up out of the ditch to Molly, Early following. Early got in the saddle first. After he got his left boot out of the stirrup, Divine put his in and levered up behind Early, and Molly started off.

"So," Divine said to the back of Early's shoulder, "what's a cowboy like you doing out here at night?"

"Riding home to Manhattan."

Divine shook his head. "And I thought I was nuts. You've got fifteen miles to go yet."

"Least the storm's over. You get called out much?"

"Fair amount. When my ranch patients can't get into the office, I go to them. Couple times, I've met a patient half-way en route and treated them at the side of the road. Someday I'm gonna have to write a book about country doctoring."

The saddle leather creaked to the sway of Molly's walk.

"You know my doctor up in Manhattan," Early asked, "Doc Grafton?"

"Oh, yeah. He's a helluva a surgeon. He's been after me to move up to your big little city, but I like it where I am."

"How's that?"

"I'm the only doctor in town, except for Doc Emmett. He gets the four-legged patients, I get the two."

A yipping came from somewhere ahead. Early reined Molly in and stared off at the horizon.

"You got something there, Mister Early?"

"A pack of prairie wolves. They're stalking something." Early aimed his trigger finger at them.

Divine leaned around for a better look.

At that moment, a cow came boiling up over the lip of an arroyo, bellowing, charging at the nearest predator. The wolf leaped back. It retreated, circled, the cow stamping after it. Another wolf sped in behind and sank its teeth into the cow's hock. The cow bellowed again and kicked back, sending the animal flying.

"Doc, there's a meal out there or those critters wouldn't be pestering that cow. Here's where you get off."

Divine, bewildered, slid down to the ground.

Early spurred Molly into a gallop. He swung her toward the fence, kicked her into a jump, and she flew over the barbed wire, hit the ground and raced on after the wolves, Early hollering, whooping, waving his hat.

The wolves turned toward the ruckus and as quickly spun around and ran, their tails between their hind legs.

At the arroyo, Early pulled Molly up. He jumped off and scrambled down the side to a cluster of whitefaces, one of them flopped on her side in the snow, straining, moaning, trying to squeeze out a calf. The small cow went limp, exhausted.

Early ran back up to the pastureland. He waved to Divine, waved for him to come and, without waiting, went to Molly standing spraddle-legged, breathing hard from the gallop. Early dug in a saddle bag for a short length of rope and a burlap sack. He found them, and, with the goods in hand, pulled his canvas roll down and scurried back into the arroyo.

"Whoa, there," he said in hushed tones, talking to the wild-eyed cows. "I'm only here to help."

He eased his way up to the two who had chosen to stand guard over their sister on the ground, talking to them, reassuring them, patting their shoulders. He squeezed between them. When Early got clear of them, he knelt by the cow on the ground, by her rear. The muscles of her body seized in another contraction to expel the calf from her birth canal. A pair of translucent hooves appeared, but nothing more as again she went limp.

"Lady," Early whispered, "you are in one big bucket of trouble."

Divine appeared at the top of the arroyo. "What's going on down there?"

"We've got a little heifer here trying her best to become a momma. The calf's hung up. It's killing her. How are your cow-doctoring skills?"

"Less than the proverbial hill of beans."

"Well, get down here and I'll give you a lesson."

"Those cows, they don't look none too friendly."

"With the wolves gone, they'll settle down. Just come down here with your best bedside manner."

Divine hesitated. After some moments, he came sliding down the side of the arroyo. "Hey, bossy. Hey, bossy," he said as he neared the guard cows. Keeping his hands to himself, he sidled between the cows to Early.

The muscles of the cow on the ground wound up for another contraction. She moaned long with the hard effort to birth her calf, straining, and went limp again when the contraction released.

She huffed for air.

Divine pushed his cap onto the back of his head. "That calf's hung up, all right."

Early looked up at him. "Cesarean, Doc?"

"Are you nuts? We could never make this area sterile."

"We can cut the calf out."

"And kill the cow, yes. Have you shoved your hand up her butt to see what's going on?"

"I've been waiting for you."

"Well, I'm not gonna do it."

"No, you're gonna assist. Get down here."

Divine, grumbling, knelt.

Early, out of his duster and sheepskin, held up his hank of rope. "See here," he said, and looped the rope around the hooves sticking out of the heifer's vulva. "You hold onto the rope. If I can get the calf loose, you pull it out."

Early pushed his shirt sleeve and underwear sleeve up to his shoulder. He eased his hand into the heifer's vulva, working his fingers along the calf's front legs, feeling his way. "Oh, damn, her head's turned back. I'm gonna have to push the calf back in and get that head turned around."

Early, on his side, shoved, straining, grimacing, until his arm was inside the heifer up to his shoulder.

He hooked his fingers in the corner of the calf's mouth and pulled, pulled the head around, the calf sucking on his fingers—an automatic response, to Early a pleasing response. "We've got us a live one here, Doc. Tug a little bit on the rope, now. Let's get her back in the canal."

Divine pulled, and the rope began to inch out, Early's arm with it. "Whoa, now, we've got it now."

Early extracted his arm. He got to his knees and from there sat back on his haunches. With the sack, he toweled the wet slickness off his arm and hand. "On the next series of contractions, Doc, it's up to you. Pull 'er out."

Moments passed with Divine focused on the rope. A contraction hit the heifer hard, all the muscles squeezing, the heifer moaning. Divine pulled with the prolonged contraction. The hooves appeared. On the next contraction, the legs showed. The next, the muzzle. On the fourth, the calf's head up to its eyes. On the fifth, the shoulders. The sixth, the barrel of the middle. On the seventh, the calf slid out of the heifer, the umbilical cord breaking free.

Early toweled the calf down.

The calf's sides heaved, and it hauled in a breath.

Early chuckled as he swaddled the calf in the canvas. "That's the way, baby. Haul in that fresh air."

Behind them, with another contraction the afterbirth flushed out of the heifer. She, free of the birthing effort, swung her head up and back, her eyes searching for her calf. Early brought it to her, and she licked at the calf's face.

"Can you get up, girl?" he said. With the calf in his arms, Early backed away from the heifer. "Come on, come on now."

She struggled up, wobbling, stood for a moment, then staggered toward Early. He laid the calf down, and she licked its face again and again, lowing at the calf.

"Doc, we can't leave the little one and her momma out here as weak as they are or they'll be critter food for sure. We've got to take 'em with us to the W-Bar, get 'em in a barn out of the weather. What is it, another mile or so?"

"That's what I'd guess."

Early pulled his sleeves down and went for his sheepskin. "Let's get a move on."

A STRAGGLY PARADE made its way into the ranch yard as the eastern sky pinked up, Molly with Divine in the saddle, the swaddled calf laying across the horse's withers, and Early walking. Behind him came the heifer and the two guard cows behind her, both glancing back as if they were checking for wolves.

At the barn, Early led the parade inside, the barn rich with the dusty smell of prairie hay. He deposited the new momma and her calf in one stall, the guard cows in another, and Molly in a third. While he pulled Molly's saddle off, the door opened a second time.

"Thought I heard someone," a woman said.

Divine went to the new arrival and her dog, a mottled creature with a stub tail, Divine with his hand out. "Nan, I'm sorry I'm late. Got stuck in the ditch last night. How's your sister?"

"In a heap of pain."

"I'll go see what I can do. Can you take care of my partner?" Divine pointed the ranch woman to Early coming out of Molly's stall, then dashed away.

Early motioned for the ranch woman to join him at the heifer's stall. "I'm James Early. We've brought you a Christmas present."

Nan Taylor, built square and close to the ground and with a scar reaching from her ear to her chin, leaned on the half door. She gazed at the cow, on the small side, and her calf, the calf standing, nursing.

Her dog came over. He put his paws up on the door and watched the cow and calf, Taylor stroking the dog's head.

"Ma'am," Early said, "I've not seen a dog like that one before. What kind is he?"

"An Aussie." She riffled the dog's ears. "Good old Royal Albert Winston, that's what we call him. Well, really we just call him Roy. He's our ranch hand."

"A stock dog?"

"Great herder." Taylor brought her hands together, as if in prayer, motioning with her fingertips to the calf. "When was the little one born?"

"Couple hours ago. The prairie wolves were hanging around, so I thought it best to bring them in."

She turned her face toward Early. "I thank you. Willa and I always worry about these winter babies. By the way, I'm Nan Taylor."

She stuck her hand out.

Early shook it. "Willa? That your daughter?"

"My sister. My senior sister. This is our ranch, Mister Early. I'm the N of the W-Bar-N."

Early pushed his cattleman's hat over one eyebrow, a la Will Rogers. "And the W is—"

"That's right."

Early thumbed back toward Molly's stall. "Can I get some water for my horse? She hasn't had any since yesterday morning. I think she's kinda parched."

"Oh, sure. The pump's just outside the door. There's a bucket just inside with a little water to prime it. I'll fork some hay in the bunks for your horse and the cows while you pump away."

Early hitched up his trousers and made his way outside with the bucket. He found the pump right where Taylor said it would be. Why, he thought, hadn't I noticed it on the way in? Well, I guess I had other things on my mind.

He poured the water into the pump, set the bucket under the spout, and went to working the pump handle, metal on metal squalling inside the pumping mechanism with each stroke. A half-minute in, the first splash of water reached the top of the well and spilled into the bucket. Another half-minute of sweaty work and Early had the bucket full.

He toted it inside, taking care not to slosh any water into his boots. Early swung the bucket up and over the half door of Molly's stall and lowered it to the floor.

She came away from the feed bunk dragging a mouthful of prairie hay with her. Molly chewed and swallowed and whiffled at Early.

"Go to it, girl," he said.

She plunged her muzzle into the bucket, sucking up the water, swallow by swallow.

Taylor and her dog came over. She leaned on her pitchfork. "Right good-looking horse you've got there."

"Yeah, she's special." Early rubbed Molly between her ears and up along the top of her mane. "Lost her a couple years ago when I had to sell my ranch. Just got to buy her back yesterday."

"Christmas present for yourself?"

"Guess you could say that."

"So where you bound for?"

"Manhattan."

Taylor hung her pitchfork on a nail. "You've got some ride yet. How about we get you to the house. We can check on Doc and Sis, and I'll make you some breakfast."

"Can't say no to that."

Once outside, Early couldn't hold it back anymore. He peered at Taylor from the corner of his eye, she as bundled against the weather as he, her dog lazing along at her side. "So, what happened to your sister, anyway?"

"Well, yesterday we were bringing our bull in from winter pasture, and he didn't take too kindly to being taken away from his cows. He charged Sis on her horse and crushed her ankle. By the time I got her to the house, her ankle had swelled so much I had to cut her boot off." She showed the size of the swelling with her gloved hands, the size about the circumference of a softball.

Early shook his head.

Taylor tickled her dog's ear as they continued on. "So there I was with a heckuva mess, Mister Early. That's why I called Doc. He said it'd be easier for him to come out than for me to wrestle Sis into the truck and drive to town."

They stepped up onto the porch where they kicked the snow from their boots. Taylor pointed her dog to a nest of hay beside the door. He went to it and turned a couple circles in the center before he flopped down.

Early opened the door for Taylor, then followed her in, stripping himself out of his coats and his chaps. Noting her lead, he hung everything on pegs beside the door.

Divine came out of a side room. He raked his fingers back through his hair. "I'm not sure what we've got here," he said to Taylor. "Might be a broken ankle. Might be just one terrible big sprain. All that swelling, I can't feel the bones, and me prodding around has your sister yelling at me with language I'd never expect from a school teacher."

Taylor glanced at Early. "Sis teaches in the one-room school on the next ranch."

Early motioned to a chair by the fireplace. He got a nod from Taylor and sat down. He pulled off a boot, the leather wet. "You could do with an X-ray, huh, Doc?"

"Except the nearest machine is in Manhattan, at the hospital, and I'm betting the road between here and there is pretty well plugged."

Early pulled off his other boot. At last, he parked his stockinged feet close to the fire to roast.

Divine came over. He sniffed the air. "A little Doctor Scholl's powder would take care of that foot stink."

Early frowned up at him.

"Anyway," Divine said, "the only thing I can think to do for Willa is splint that ankle—keep it immobile. Nan will have to ice it to get the swelling down. Nan, you got any ice in the house?"

"I can bust some out of the stock tank."

"Good. Got something we can make a couple splints out of?"

"Some wood in our shop out in the barn."

"Excellent. You get a bucket of ice chunks we can break up, and, Mister Early, how about you get out there and make us some splints?"

Early sighed. Still he pulled on his boots and sheepskin and hustled to the barn. There, out of habit, he checked on the livestock in their stalls—the guard cows lounging, the momma and her calf laying down, the momma cow grooming her calf's face with her tongue. And Molly at the feed bunk, still feasting on prairie hay.

At the far end of the barn, Early opened a door to a room on the right, a tack room he discovered with harnesses and saddles hung up and bags of grain piled in a corner. He could smell the leather dressing used to keep the harnesses soft.

He went across the alley to the room on the opposite side. He opened the door and, without looking in, knew from the smell of sawdust that he had found the wood shop—fresh sawdust, not old dry sawdust. That told him the sisters must have been building something. He saw it on a workbench, a cabinet likely destined for the kitchen, the wood not yet stained or painted.

Early found a scrap barrel. He poked around in it and came up with a couple lengths of one-by-twos and one-by-threes. He liked the one-by-threes better for no particular reason. Early laid them on the bench and went scrounging in a drawer for sandpaper, found some, and sanded the edges of the pieces until he had them rounded and smooth. No splinters. No snags.

He placed one of the pieces against his leg, the bottom part at his heel, and estimated about ten inches would be the right length. Early took down a crosscut saw. He sawed the first piece off and held it against his leg again. Uh-huh, he thought, that'll do.

Next, Early sanded the ends, then laid the finished piece on the scrap he had left. He marked it for cutting.

Early set the saw's teeth against the board for the start of the new cut. He drew the saw back and pushed it forward, the teeth biting into the wood, spitting out the small bits—the dust. On an upstroke, the saw struck a knot and jumped out of the cut. It raked across Early's thumb, ripping into the flesh.

Early yelped.

He dropped the saw and whipped out his bandana. Early wrapped his thumb. He finished the cut in anger at himself and ran for the house. Early charged through the front room, into the side room where Divine and Willa Taylor sat talking, Taylor lying on the bed, her foot propped up on a pillow. Early thrust the splints at Divine.

Divine ran his hand over the pieces. "Nice. Very nice. But what's this red stain here on the end?" He glanced up at Early, at the wrapping on his thumb. "What the hell, did you cut yourself?"

Early laid the bandana open. "Since you're a doc—"

"Oh, for Lordy sake." Divine hauled Early to a side table on which rested a porcelain basin half-filled with water. "Willa, this clumsy clod is James Early."

Early nodded to her, by her length taller than her sister, slender and raw-boned, her face weathered, carved by the prairie winds. He couldn't see any student wanting to smart off to her.

Divine plunged Early's hand into the water. He worked his fingers around the bloody tear, cleaning the wound. Divine brought the hand out. He inspected the thumb in the light from a kerosene lamp. "The good news, Mister Early, you'll live. Stick your hand back in the water while I get the gauze and some alcohol."

Early did as instructed. When Divine returned, he laid out a wealth of stuff—a roll of gauze, two small bottles, one of alcohol and the other of a reddish liquid. Early recognized that one—mercurochrome—knew he was in for pain for sure.

Divine also laid out a towel, a band-aide still in its sterile packaging, a syringe, and another even smaller bottle.

All for a cut thumb? Early thought that seemed like overkill.

Divine lifted Early's hand from the water. He patted it dry with the towel, blood still oozing from the cut. Divine splashed the cut with alcohol.

Early cringed.

Divine held up the bottle. "Maybe you'd rather drink it."

"I'm tempted."

Divine set the bottle aside. He wrapped Early's thumb with gauze. "When the bleeding stops, I'll put mercurochrome and a band-aide on it."

Early tilted his head toward the syringe.

Divine picked it up. "Oh, this? Wonderful thing. Drop your britches."

"What?"

"I'm gonna give you a tetanus shot."

"Here? In front of her?" Early waved his hand with the wrapped thumb at the woman in the bed.

"She can turn her head away if she wants. Drop your britches."

"All because of a little cut?"

"Do it!"

Early, smoldering, unbuckled his belt. He turned his back to Divine, pulled his jeans down, and unbuttoned the back flap of his long red underwear. Hardly done, he felt a sharp jab in his right glute. Early bit his lip.

"Done," Divine said.

Nan Taylor burst in with a dishpan of crushed ice as Early rebuttoned his back flap. "Did I miss something?" she asked.

Divine showed her the syringe. "Tetanus shot in the hiny for our wounded carpenter. I've got enough juice left for you and Willa."

"We're current. You shot us both up last year, when I had my tangle with the barbed wire." She drew her fingers down the scar on the side of her face.

"Well, let's get your sister splinted up. It's going to take the three of us."

Willa Taylor stared at the trio. "At last, I'm going to get some attention."

Divine glanced at her. "You weren't bleeding, so you could wait."

"Well, I never—"

"Willa, nothing gained by working yourself up in a huff." He positioned the splints. "Nan, you lift your sister's leg. Mister Early and I will do the rest."

As she did, Divine nodded for Early to take the splints.

Early got his hands on them.

Divine brought an elastic bandage out of his bag. He wrapped the bandage around the splinted ankle and lower leg. Divine shot a look at Nan Taylor as he worked. "You have a hot water bottle?"

"Two. Actually."

"Excellent. Fill them both with crushed ice. When you have that done, pack them around your sister's ankle."

Nan Taylor went to the bureau opposite the bed. She brought a hot water bottle out of one of the drawers and proceeded to fill the bottle with ice.

Divine placed Willa Taylor's splinted ankle and foot back on the pillow. "You don't complain much, do you?"

She brushed the hair back from her forehead. "Learned long ago that doesn't accomplish much."

"It doesn't, does it? Have any breakfast, yet?"

"Hours ago," Willa Taylor said. "Unlike you, we ranch people are early risers."

Divine leaned an elbow on the headboard. He gazed down at his patient. "Any chance Mister Early and I could rustle up something in your kitchen? It's been a long time since either of us has had a meal. I can't speak for Mister Early, but my stomach's gnawing on my ribs."

EARLY PUSHED his plate aside while Nan Taylor refilled his coffee cup. "Have you ever been Santa Claus?" she asked.

"Pardon?"

She went on to Divine's cup. "Santa Claus. We've got a tradition. Christmas morning, all of Willa's students and their parents come over to our place, and Santa comes and gives each child a present."

Early warmed his hands over his cup. "And you want me to do that?"

"Mister Early, I'm usually Santa Claus. Most of the kids know it. But wouldn't it be a surprise to them if Santa came in and I'm here in the room?"

"'Fraid I don't have the build or the beard, ma'am."

"I've got the whiskers and the Santa suit. When you've togged yourself up, you stuff a pillow halfway down the front of your red britches and you've got a belly."

Divine winked at Early from across the table. "Do it or I'll call Doctor Grafton and tell him you need a tetanus booster shot, that he should use his rusty needle."

Sleigh bells jingled outside.

Nan Taylor hustled to the window. "Oh, lordy, the first family's here already, and there's more coming up the lane. What do you say, Mister Early, is it you or me?"

Divine horsed Early up out of his chair. "It's him."

Early pulled his arm away. "Gee, thanks, Doc."

"What are you, a Scrooge? The surprised looks on the faces of those youngsters, you might get a hug or two."

Nan Taylor went to a closet. She brought out two well-stuffed pillowcases and a Christmas-wrapped package a couple feet long by a foot wide. Taylor handed them to Early. "One pillowcase's got the beard and suit, the other the presents. So's this big package. Now let's get your coats and hat, and you go out the back door. Mister Early, run to the barn so no one sees you. You can change there."

EARLY, in the tack room, stepped into the red trousers. He held the waist out, sure big enough for a pillow or a pillow and a half. Early peered around the room. She hadn't given him a pillow, but he spotted a bunch of empty grain sacks. Early wadded them together. He stuffed them into his reds and followed that by cinching up a belt to hold them, a belt with a silver buckle he had found in the pillowcase. The buckle, he ran his fingers over the raised letters on it.

Early twisted the buckle up, the better to read what it said: State Champion Calf Roper, 1943.

Nan Taylor's buckle?

A woman winning the state calf-roping championship?

How come I didn't know that, he wondered. Of course, State Fair time for the rodeo—the first week of September—I was in Italy, up in the mountains with the Rangers, out to kill a German artillery unit shelling the Brits on the Salerno beach. Oh, well, that was then. Kids are waiting.

Early pulled on the red coat and looped the beard's elastics over his ears.

But the Santa hat, he puzzled about that. Leave his sweat-stained cattleman's hat behind?

No, he thought, and instead fitted the Santa hat over the crown of his cattleman's hat. Early glanced at himself in a glass. Yup, he thought, wiggling his fingers at his image, looks right for a cowboy Santa.

Early poked the gifts, except for the big one, into his saddlebags and toted them, the package, and his tack to Molly's stall. On a post next to the door, he found a strap of harness bells. Early added the bells to his collection and opened the door.

Molly pulled back, fear in her eyes.

Early yanked his beard down. "Come on, you know me, old girl."

Her eyes warmed. She whinnied and came to him, pushed her face into his chest.

"Yah, you're a good old soul." Early rubbed the side of her face. He slipped the bit into her mouth and the bridle up over her ears. Next, he threw a blanket across Molly's back and followed that with the saddle and all its gear. Early pulled the cinch tight. He secured it and led her outside. There he mounted up.

Early maneuvered Molly through the gaggle of pickup trucks and cars that clogged the yard between the barn and the ranch house, shaking the strap of bells as he went.

Nan Taylor and a cluster of children boiled out onto the porch, some of the children pointing, others waving, Taylor snapping pictures with a Brownie Kodak.

Early, holding the big package by the strings that bound it, stepped down from the saddle.

"It's Santa Claus," one of the girls whispered to a smaller one.

He beckoned to an older boy. "Wanna help me?"

The boy grinned.

Early laid his bulging saddle bags over the boy's shoulder, and together they went into the house, the children following them into the over-sized front room, to a cedar tree decorated with candles and red and green paper chains, a silver star at the top.

Early settled on a ladderback chair. He set his package on the floor, then took his saddlebags from the boy and laid them across his knee. "All right, now all of Miss Taylor's students, I want you to line up in front of me."

A half dozen shuffled away from their parents. As they did, Nan Taylor slipped up behind Early.

He grubbed in his saddlebag for a package, brought it out, and read the tag. "Aron?"

Taylor whispered behind Early's ear, "Second left."

He beckoned to the boy, by his size the youngest of the group. The boy came forward.

Early gave him the gift.

The boy took it with one hand. With the other, he snatched at Early's beard.

Early blocked him. He leaned into him, nose to nose. "Pull my beard, son, your gift turns to coal."

Aron scrunched his face. At a motion from Early, he stepped back.

Early read the next tag. "Dessa."

"On the right," Taylor whispered.

Early pointed at the girl.

She twisted her way forward, blushing. "Is it a doll?"

Early ran his fingers over the wrapping.

"Yes," Taylor whispered.

Early nodded.

The girl gave him a shy smile. "You got my letter then."

He handed the package on. "Yes, and it was a very nice letter."

She, hugging the package, danced her way to two adults Early took to be her parents.

He bobbled the next package, catching it before it hit the floor. Early blew out his cheeks. "Close," he said and peered at the tag. "This one's for someone named Jane."

"On the right," came the whisper.

Early tipped his brow toward the girl. "Jane, I think this is something you're gonna like."

"Thank you," she said and took the package to Willa Taylor, comfortable in a soft chair, her splinted ankle up on a stool. "Is this what I think it is?"

Willa Taylor cupped her hand behind the girl's head. "Yes, it is, honey."

"You'll teach me how to knit?"

"Of course."

Early glanced at the three remaining student, all boys. He brought out a flat package. "I can tell this sure isn't a baseball and a glove."

Several of the men chuckled.

Early thumbed the tag. "This is for Eldridge."

"Center." A whisper.

He motioned the boy forward and presented him with the gift.

Early then brought out a square package about eight inches by eight inches, and he lifted the big package by its strings. "These are the last two, just right because we've got two students left. This big one is for Dwight." Early held the package out to the boy on the right.

"How'd you know?" Nan Taylor buzzed.

Early buzzed back, "Just guessed."

The boy named Dwight collected his gift and toted it to a couple, the woman cradling a baby in her arms. "What do you think it is?" she asked.

Early waved the last boy in and held out the square package to him. "Merry Christmas, Cal."

"Thank you." The boy held up the package for everyone to see, grinning a gap-toothed grin to all.

Nan Taylor clapped her hands. "All right, now. Everyone, you can open your gift."

Five peeled away the wrapping paper with the utmost of care, Early guessing they probably wanted their teacher to be able to use the paper again next Christmas.

Aron, though, ripped into his package. He held up a truck, a truck with a Tonka label on it.

"Nice," Early said when he saw it.

Nan Taylor turned him toward the other boys and motioned toward the closest. "We gave Eldridge there a sketch pad and colored pencils. He's always drawing, and he's pretty good. And Cal over yon, that's a microscope he's unwrapping. Willa has him hooked on science."

Early aimed his trigger finger at the one named Dwight holding a junior-sized guitar out to his parents.

Nan Taylor grinned. "Yes, he's always pestering me to play my guitar, so we found that beginner's one in the Sears catalog. I'll give him lessons."

Aron marched up, his hands jammed against his hips. "Santa, I wanted a big truck like my dad's, not a toy truck."

Early jacked up an eyebrow. "Aren't you a little small for a big truck?"

"Am not." He flashed out his foot in a sharp kick to Santa's shin and ran.

Early grimaced. He glanced at Taylor. "You suppose you could send him home with a lump or two of coal?"

The boy's father sidled over. "Santa, I'm sorry. My boy's a handful. I'll warm his fanny when we get him home."

"My dad did that to me more than a couple times when I was about Aron's age. By the way, I'm not Santa Claus."

"I know. Willa told me you're the sheriff of Riley County."

Early rubbed at his shin. "Yah, yah, that's me."

"Maybe I could bring Aron up to Manhattan. You could show him your jail, put him in the lockup, maybe scare him some."

Early straightened up. "I'm sorry, Mister—"

"Johnson. Riley Johnson."

"Mister Johnson, that I don't go in for. Now if you'll excuse me, I really need to be gettin' on. My horse is waiting." Early backed toward the door. "Miss Taylor, I'll leave the suit in the barn."

She slipped her arm through his and guided him outside, into the air still crisp but warmed some in the past hour. "Mister Early, this all was fun for Willa and me, you being Santa Claus. We thank you."

"Least I could do I guess after that breakfast feast. You'll send the doctor home?"

"He says he wants to see Willa settled back in the bed before he leaves. Mister Early, why don't you keep the suit and beard for the time? Wear it on your ride north."

Early shook his head.

"Do it. Consider the looks on people's faces when they see you, Santa Claus, riding through Manhattan on a horse on Christmas Day. I'd like to see that myself, but—"

"But you've got a sister and a ranch to look after." Early rubbed behind his ear, giving himself a moment of thinking time. "Tell you what, I'm not much of a joker, Miss Taylor, but what you propose, that's interesting. Now your suit and beard, suppose I bring them back sometime and see how you and your sister are gettin' on."

EARLY, STIFFENING UP, wondered how long he had been riding, a couple hours, he thought, when the snorting of a diesel motor somewhere ahead interrupted his mental meanderings. He reined Molly to a stop.

A half a football field on, a road grader topped a rise and came huffing down the lee side, its V-plow peeling snow off toward the ditches as it cleaved a single lane through the drifts. The grader driver, his conveyance closing the distance, wig-wagged to Early. "Ho, there, Santa! Ain't you supposed to be home by now?"

"Will be before long." Early doffed his cattleman's hat topped with his loaner Santa hat to the driver as the man wheeled his big yellow machine by.

The driver waved again. "Good to see ya, man. My wife's not gonna believe this."

Early watched the grader go on over the next rise. The beeping of a car's horn brought him back.

Rolling along the newly opened track came a bullet-nosed Ford pulling a horse trailer, a Kansas State Police shield on the door of the car. The rig stopped abreast of Early.

The driver's window cranked down, and a state trooper stuck his head out. "Jimmy, that you?"

Early leaned on the pommel of his saddle, Molly nodding, blasting her nostrils clear. "Well, if it isn't Daniel Plemmons. What're you doin' out here?"

"Looking for you. You've been reported missing. Can I give you and your horse a ride home?"

Early popped his thumb up. He spurred Molly out of the ditch and around to the back of the trailer where, after he stepped down, he opened the gate. Molly, no stranger to horse trailers, hefted herself inside.

Plemmons, too, shambled around. He put his hand on the gate before Early could close it. "Jimmy, you should have called me rather than Clovis Henthorn. I would have taken you down to the Grove and hauled your horse back for you, avoided all this trouble."

A smile pushed up the ends of Early's mustache. He pulled off his Santa hat and held it in his gloved hands. "Trouble? Daniel, you won't believe the Christmas I've had out here."

Note: Sometimes a Christmas miracle comes about because you know the right person. This is one of those stories.

The Least of These

JAMES EARLY slogged away from his Jeep, Doc Grafton, the county coroner, humping along beside him, both men with their collars turned up and their hats pulled low against the wind and snow.

Grafton rammed his hands deeper in his overcoat pockets. "Not the best morning to be out, Cactus."

"Could be worse. Could be tomorrow. Messed up your Christmas."

"You wouldn'tna got me."

"How's that?"

"The boss and me, tomorrow morning we're in Strong City, she helping Gramma make breakfast and me with my feet propped up by the fire in the kitchen stove."

"I do hope you get there."

They pushed on and up beside two men hunched like horses, their backsides to the wind, one—Mose

Dickerson, the Riley constable and the area's mail carrier—stamping his feet, the other—Wilton Brown, the undertaker—huffing his breath into his gloved hands. Beyond them, four others pitched snow, shoveling their way through the ditch, toward a wrecked pickup and a busted-off power pole.

Early sidled up beside Dickerson. "What've we got here, Mose?"

He stopped stamping. "Lights along here went out about daybreak, Jimmy. People, they jumped on the party line and finally got through to the R.E.A., to see what the trouble was. That's why Milty and Gordy are out here."

"They found the wreck?"

"And the mess with the pole and the power line."

"You?"

Dickerson went to stamping his feet again. "I was comin' by on my mail route, so I stopped. Milty'd already radioed back for a wrecker and Brownie with his meat wagon. An' you, of course."

"Dead one, huh?"

"Milty says so." Dickerson adjusted his ear muffs, the better to keep the skin on the back of his ears from freezing. "I looked in the cab. Gotta agree."

"Know who it is?"

"Face is busted up, but, yeah. That old truck with no rear fenders, that's Eldon Treat's, so that's gotta be Eldon inside."

"Do I know him?"

"Not likely, Jimmy. The Treats is new around here, an' Eldon, he works over in Clay. Probably where he was goin' when he lost it in the snow."

Early peered over at the second man. "This weather to your liking, Brownie?"

"Wouldn't give you a diddly darn for it."

"Think you can get the body out of that wreck?"

"Not by myself. Milty's gonna cut the door off for me with his torch, maybe the steering wheel post, too. The deader's pinned in there like a butterfly in a display case."

"Well, I brought Doc up here to make it official, so—" Early shrugged. He pushed off into the ditch, a gloved hand on his work-stained cattleman's hat to keep it from blowing away.

Grafton, as he moved along with Early, pitched his muffler over the crown of his fedora. He pulled the ends of his muffler down, making the brim of his hat work like ear flaps.

They hustled on past the shoveling crew—the wrecker drivers and the two R.E.A. linemen—widening their path so they could back the tow truck down into the ditch and up to the crash.

Grafton nudged Early on. "Let's get this done before I turn into a popsicle."

They hopped from the end of the hand-dug trail into snow up to their knees.

Early grabbed hold of the side of the truck box and pulled himself along. When he got to the driver's door, he ran his hand up and over the frame. "It's pinched in, all right. Impact busted out all the glass, so, Doc, you can reach in for a pulse."

Grafton elbowed Early out of the way. He shucked off a glove and stuck his bare hand in the cab, to the body. He worked his fingertips under a collar, to the carotid artery. Grafton pressed in and held his fingertips there for a moment.

He shook his head. "That's all she wrote." Grafton glanced at his watch. "I hereby confirm the obvious at the hour of eight thirty-two in the a.m. This man's dead. Jimmy, let's get back to your Jeep. I wanna thaw my fingers."

Early made an about-face, Grafton with him. They high-stepped back through the deep snow to the ditch and up to Dickerson and Brown, Brown now in the cab of his Black Mariah, Dickerson by the door, he again stamping in the snow.

Early rapped on the glass.

Brown rolled the window down.

"Brownie, Doc's made the death official. The body's yours."

"You want me to get in touch with the family?"

"I'll do that. But I'll tell you it's the one part of my job I do hate."

"Understand."

Early spun his pointer finger in a gesture for the undertaker to roll his window up. Next, he guided Dickerson by the elbow to the constable's car, an old Chevy coupe, a stovebolt six, the paint sun bleached. "So there is a wife?"

"And two little kids. The wife, from the one time I met her at the post office, she's one sour apple."

"Where's the house?"

"Couple miles back into Riley. I can take you there. You wanna follow me?"

EARLY STOPPED behind Dickerson's car. He glanced at Grafton in the buddy seat, then past him to the house. "Not much, is it?"

Grafton cast his gaze that way. "Kind of like the hovel the boss and I had when we first came to Manhattan, three rooms and a path. Wouldn't want it today for a chicken coop."

"I remember it. Well, come on." Early stepped out of the Jeep.

Grafton came out the other side. Together they kicked their way through the snow to the front stoop, Dickerson hop-stepping to keep up.

Early rapped on the door frame. When no one answered, he rapped again. This time the door opened a crack, enough that he could see a sliver of a woman on the other side, a woman in a tired house dress, her face, what Early could see of it, deeply lined.

She raised an eyebrow, as if suspicious of something. "Whaddya you want?"

"Missus Treat?"

"Yeah?"

"I'm Sheriff Early. Can my friends and I come in and talk?"

"If this has got somethin' to do with Eldon, he's not here."

"It does."

"Then it'll have to wait. He's at work. Be home tonight."

"I'm sorry, Missus Treat, he won't be."

"You sayin' somethin' happened?" Her hand went to her mouth, and she retreated a pace.

Early sensed an advantage. He eased the door open. He stepped inside, into a dingy room smelling of coal oil and Vicks VapoRub. Early went in far enough that Grafton and Dickerson could slip in behind him. Both snatched off their hats, Dickerson his ear muffs, too.

Early shifted his weight. "Your mailman here tells me you've got kids."

"Two. Not mine so much as Eldon's." Missus Treat snuffled. She wiped at her nose with a handkerchief that was hardly more than a rag.

"Where are they?"

"In the kitchen, feedin' their faces." She wiped at her nose again. "Don't you look at me accusing. Breakfast's kinda late today."

Early motioned to Grafton, for him to go on to the kitchen. As he left, Early sat down on one of the two hard-backed chairs in the room. Missus Treat, her stare following Grafton, hesitated before she, too, sat down.

Early removed his hat. He glanced around. "I see you've not got your Christmas tree up yet?"

"Don't believe in that stuff."

"That so? Well—" Early leaned forward, his elbows coming to rest on his knees. "—ma'am, there's no easy way to put this."

"Put this what?"

"Your husband, ma'am, he ran off the road on his way to work it looks like, hit an electric pole."

Missus Treat's eyes took on the look of a wild animal suddenly boxed it.

He went on. "Wilton Brown—he's our undertaker in Manhattan—he's out there. He'll take care of your husband."

She choked back what, words? Tears? Early couldn't be sure which. "Is there any way we can help you, Missus Treat?"

She rose, decidedly, firmly. She planted her hand on the back of her chair, the rag of a handkerchief showing between her fingers, a fierceness firing her face. "Help?"

"Yes, ma'am."

"You kin help, sheriff. You kin take them children. They're not mine. Take 'em or I'll put 'em out on the street. The only reason we got 'em was because Eldon was their only relative nearby when their ma and pa died of the sick they had. You get 'em outta here, and you get 'em outta here now."

EARLY, as he drove for home, the snow having ended, the sun breaking through the clouds, glanced at the boy in the seat beside him, the boy's coat and pants too short and cracks showing in the leather of his shoes. "Arland, you say you're nine?"

The boy fiddled with a thread hanging from the cuff of one sleeve of his coat. "Uh-huh."

"And your brother?" Early looked up at his mirror, at the small boy next to Grafton in the backseat, Grafton with his arm around him.

"Seven."

"Name's Merlie?"

"Uh-huh."

"I notice he doesn't talk. Is that because we're strangers?"

"Huh-uh."

"What then?"

"Ma Treat."

"What about Ma Treat?"

"She, uhm, whipped him."

"Whipped him?"

"Uh-huh."

"Why?"

"He asked for a second potato at supper once."

"Once?"

"He cried, so she whipped him again, for crying."

"Wasn't Mister Treat there?"

"Huh-uh."

Early's thoughts tumbled. Beating an older kid, he'd known that to happen, but a child? After some moments, he forced out a question, "When was this?"

"Sometime back, after they got us."

"She ever whip you?"

"Uh-huh. She'd make me drop my pants, switch my bottom if I wouldn't do something she wanted."

Early blew out his breath, his cheeks looking like those of a chipmunk. He turned the Jeep off onto the lane that led to a ranch house and barns. Early again glanced at the boy. "That's not going to happen to you or Merlie anymore."

"Mister Early, can I ask you a question?"

"Sure."

"What's gonna happen to us? My brother and me, we got no home."

"The home you had wasn't much." Early guided the Jeep down a dip and across the ice of a frozen creek that in spring and fall washed across the lane. "Arland, I'm going to work on that. You've got my promise. But for now, how about you two fellas spending Christmas with me and the people I live with and my little girl? Would that be all right?"

The boy didn't look up. He instead stared at his shoes, but Early could see a hint of a smile.

As they neared the buildings, a black dog—a Newfoundland—raced out from one of the barns toward the Jeep, throwing up snow as he ran, the dog flailing his tail.

"That's Archie," Early said. "You and Merlie are gonna like him."

"I had a dog once."

"When was that?"

"When I was little. Merlie doesn't remember him."

"Your brother's of a size I could saddle old Arch and he could ride him." Early looked to the boy for a laugh, but none came. He swung the Jeep around in the ranch yard and stopped by the front porch of a low-slung house, smoke drifting up from its two chimneys. Archie, outside the passenger's window, pressed his nose against the plastic, his eyes bright, focused on the boy.

Early stepped out. He came around and slap-patted the dog. Then, with one hand, he held Archie back while, with the other, he opened the door for the boy.

The boy slid off the seat, and the dog broke loose. He danced around, licking at the boy's face, while the boy, giggling and scrunching up, tried his best to pet Archie.

Early stepped in. He grabbed the dog's collar and issued the order, "Sit!"

Archie plopped his butt in the snow.

The boy reached out to him. The dog slobbered on his hand, all the time not lifting his bottom from where he sat, yet the dog worked his tail like a broom, sweeping the snow from side to side.

Early pulled the passenger seat forward to get the smaller boy in the backseat. "Come on, Merlie."

Grafton handed the boy forward.

Early caught him and brought him out. He set the boy down on his feet next to Arland. "Merlie, I'd like you to meet Archie. He's gonna be your best buddy while you're here."

The boy, like his brother, reached out to the dog and got a bunch of raspy licks on his hand in return. He giggled.

Grafton hauled himself out of the backseat, bumping the horn button as he came. The beep brought Nadine Estes to the door, an apron around her waist and her hands well dusted with flour. She motioned to the boys with their arms wrapped around Archie's neck. "Looks like we got company here."

Early pulled a pillowcase out from the back of the Jeep, the pillowcase stuffed with clothes. "For a time, Christmas at least." He herded Arland and Merlie ahead of him and up onto the porch. Archie came beside them, sworping his tongue at Merlie. "Boys, I want you to kick the snow off your shoes before you go inside. That's Missus Estes. She looks after my little girl and me."

Merlie stamped around and Arland raked his shoes against a bootjack, both getting their foot gear somewhat clean. Early, after a wait, pushed them on inside. He then kicked the snow from his boots, and Grafton did the same with his galoshes. Following that, they thundered in to find Missus Estes helping the boys out of their coats.

She ruffled Arland's hair. "I've been baking Christmas cookies. How would you two fellers like a couple with milk?"

That brought grins.

She whisked the boys ahead of her and out of the big room well warmed by a fire in the fireplace, the air pungent with the scent of cedar from the Christmas tree in the corner.

Early parked his fanny on the hearth. There he pulled off his boots and gave his toes a vigorous rub through the fabric of his socks. "Doc, if heaven's like this—a warm house, good friends, a dog like Archie, and my horse—I won't mind going when it comes my time."

Grafton, out of his five-bucklers, set his galoshes aside. "You aren't planning on that soon, are you?"

"Nope."

The boys shuffled back in from the kitchen, Merlie carrying a plate of cookies and Arland two cups of coffee, steam rising from them. With Missus Estes pointing the way, they served Grafton first, then Early. She carried in glasses of milk which she handed to the boys after they settled on the rug in front of the fire.

She dipped her brow to Early. "Did you know these two fine young men are from Nebraska and their last name is Snyder, not Treat?"

Early waved what was left of his cookie. "That I did not. Guess I'm not too good at asking questions, am I?" He squared off to the boys. "Tell me, Mister Arland Snyder and Mister Merlie Snyder, do you have any other family, relatives like Mister Treat?"

Arland, finished with his cookies, peered at another on the plate. When he turned his gaze upward, Missus Estes was watching him.

"It's all right," she said. "Two are never enough."

With that, he helped himself to a third cookie. He passed it to his brother, then took another for himself. This one he balanced on his glass. Arland brushed his fingers on his shirt front, to get the crumbs off them, then reached inside his shirt. He brought out a leather pouch on a cord looped around his neck. From the pouch, Arland excavated an envelope, folded. "We got a sister."

Early set his coffee cup aside. "Where?"

The boy handed him the envelope.

Early unfolded it and read the return address. "Fort Hood. She in the Army?"

Arland shook his head. "The man she's married to."

Early poked his fingers inside the envelope for a letter he knew must be there. He got it, opened it, and scanned down the page. "I see. He's a sergeant.

And here your sister talks about—oh, she's got a baby."

"Uh-huh."

"You ever see the baby?"

"Huh-uh."

"Your sister, when did you see her last?"

"When Merlie was little."

"You like her and the man's she's married to?"

'Uh-huh."

Early tapped the envelope and the letter against his fingertips. "You wouldn't mind if I made a telephone call, would you?"

The boy shook his head.

Early, still tapping the envelope and the letter against his fingertips, got up and went to the kitchen. There he took down the receiver from the wall phone. He gave a long crank on the ringer, then pressed the receiver to his ear.

A voice came through. "This is the operator."

Early turned to the mouthpiece. "Betts, James Early. I need your help."

"What can I do for you, Sheriff?"

"Would you place a long-distance call for me? Fort Riley? The adjutant?"

"Do you have a number?"

"Just a minute." He thumbed through the pages of a notepad he had taken from his shirt pocket. "Here it is. Two-two-one-six."

"I have an open circuit to Fort Riley."

Early heard a ring, then a second ring. A man answered, a high tenor. "Fort Riley switchboard."

"I have a long distance call for the post adjutant. Two-two-one-six."

"Cross your fingers, ma'am, it's the day before Christmas. Putting you through now."

This time a buzz came out of the receiver, like that of an angry bee. A second buzz, and a third. And a click of a receiver being picked up.

"Adjutant here. By God, this better be important."

"Long distance call from Leonardville."

"Who the hell—"

Early shoved his way into the conversation. "Henry, it's me, James Early."

"You I'll talk to. By the way, merry Christmas and may Santa Claus not put a lump of coal in your stocking this year."

"Coal we can always use. Gets mighty chilly out on the ranch."

"Why you calling, Cactus?"

"I got two orphan boys here. I'm trying to find their sister and her husband. He's in the Army."

"One of my troopers?"

"No. Screaming Eagles at Fort Hood, a Sergeant Thomas Wills. You think you could make a couple calls and find him?"

"Cactus, you don't ask much."

"Can you do it?"

Silence. Early imagined the bird colonel was sucking on his pipe, trying to come up with a way to get out of this.

The adjutant's voice came back. "You're sure of this?"

"I'm holding a letter from the sister, Janey Wills, dated Twelve September."

"Where are you?"

"Out at the ranch. Leonardville four-one-four."

"I'll make some calls, get back to you within the hour. You know I'm probably going to have to sacrifice my lunch for you."

"Next time you come to Manhattan, I'll take you to the Brass Nickel. And I'll buy."

"Steak with all the trimmings?"

"If you find the sergeant and his wife, I'll even put half a peach pie on your plate for dessert." Early hung the receiver back on the hook.

He slipped the letter back in the envelope and folded it as he strolled back into the front room. Early held the envelope out to Arland. "You'll be wanting this."

The boy took it and returned it to his pouch.

Early turned his gaze to Missus Estes. "So where's Walter and Toot?"

"Jimmy, Walter took your little girl to Manhattan, to the Woolworth, so she can get you something for Christmas. Coming on three years old and buying you a Christmas gift. If I know my Walter, and I do, he'll see to it it's a bottle of Old Spice, so you act surprised when you open your present."

"I can do that."

"And I'll do the same when I unwrap the box of chocolate-covered cherries he'll get for me. He gets 'em so he can eat the most of 'em. Always does." She grinned as she shook her head. "Well, I better get some lunch ready for these hungry young 'uns. Maybe they'd like to see Molly while I do."

Arland looked up at Early. "Who's Molly?"

"My horse."

The boy grabbed hold of his brother's hand. "Come on, we're gonna see Mister Early's horse."

WHEN EARLY and the boys clattered back into the house, Grafton stood waiting for them in the doorway to the kitchen, an apron tied up under his arms. "Come on, you Indians, get out of your coats and get your butts in here. Missus Estes says lunch is ready and she's not going to wait but a minute more."

Early helped Merlie and Arland shed their coats, then gave them a push toward the kitchen. Grafton aimed them on, to the sink.

He swung back to Early. "Kind of like those kids, don't you?"

"Yeah, they're good all right. But I'd sure like to see them get with family for Christmas, a better family than they've had."

"You thinking that sister in Texas?"

"Yeah, blood's a powerful thing."

"My friend, don't hang your hat on that one. She's too far away."

"You're probably right." Early tugged on Grafton's apron. "Looks like you've been cooking."

"Helping. Nadine says fetch this and I do, she says do that and I get with it. I'm a right good hand when I know I'm going to be fed. Better get yourself in here."

Early went on to the sink already abandoned by the boys drying their hands on two ends of the same towel. He worked the pitcher pump, splashing new water into the sink. He plunged in and scrubbed his face while Nadine Estes settled the boys on a bench beside her plank table. She took the bench across from them and motioned Grafton to the chair at the foot of the table. That left the chair at the head. Early slid onto it after he dried his face and hands.

He took hold of Merlie's hand. "You boys say grace before meals?"

Merlie gave off a questioning look, and Arland shook his head.

"We do." Early reached for Nadine's hand and she for Grafton's. So it went around the table.

Early at last bowed. "Gracious God, this day started hard with You calling home one of Yours. But life goes on, doesn't it, and we thank You for that. And we thank You, too, for bringing these young men to be with us, to share a meal and maybe Christmas as well. Bless this food to us now, we do ask it in Your Son's name. And they all said—" In unison, Early, Missus Estes, and Grafton murmured amen.

A beat behind came a whispered amen from Arland.

Early gazed around the table at the noontime feast. He clapped his hands. "Well, now, what do we have?"

Missus Estes lifted a bowl of mashed potatoes to Grafton and gestured for him to pass it to Arland. "We have mashed potatoes, hot biscuits, a beef roast that I had in the oven, and corn and beans that I canned from my garden."

The telephone rang, interrupting. Early signaled for all to keep passing the dishes and dig in while he abandoned his chair for the phone. He pressed the receiver to his ear. "James Early."

"I have a long distance call from Fort Riley."

"Put it through."

Several clicks and a hum came across the line, plus, "Fort Riley, I have your party for you. Go ahead."

"Jimmy?"

Early put his hand on the stem of the mouthpiece. "Henry, I'm here. What did you find out?"

"Well, Sergeant Wills really does exist. I got him through a field phone connection. He and his squad are out on maneuvers."

"So?"

"Here's the good news. The sergeant says he and his wife would like to have the boys."

"All right."

"But bad news comes with it."

"What's that?"

"The earliest he can get a pass so they can drive up here is three weeks from now."

"Henry, that's not so bad."

"Well, maybe. Anyway, I made some more calls for you. You remember from your war days, we've got the Military Air Transport Service—MATS? They've got a bird in the air for Fort Hood that they can divert here. It's a tight schedule. Can you pack those kids and be at the Manhattan airport in twenty?"

"Twenty minutes?"

"Yeah."

Grafton glanced up from his cutting of a bite of beef.

Early motioned an 'ignore me' to him and turned his back to his company, to face full to the wall phone. "Henry, the best I can do is forty and that's with running my siren which doesn't work. But how about this? It's as illegal as all get out, but still and all—"

"Jimmy, you'd violate the law?"

"Look at your map. Fifteen miles northwest of Manhattan, Seventy-Seven curves and goes due north. From that curve, it runs straight for most of the next ten miles and most of the first part of that road is flat. We block off a mile and make it a runway and have the MATS flight land on it. That curve, it's only five miles from me."

"Jimmy, you got the vehicles to pull this off?"

"I can get a couple cars."

"Not good enough, my friend. Tell you what you need, you need some honkin' big bruisers, and I'm the man who's got 'em. Twenty minutes. Get your fanny in gear."

The adjutant clicked off.

Early hung his receiver back onto its hook. He rubbed his ear, wondering what he's just committed himself to do. While still considering it, he eased around to find everyone at the table staring at him. Early looked straight at the brothers. "Boys, how would you like to be with your sister and her family in Texas for Christmas?"

A smile lifted Arland's face. He slipped an arm around his brother's shoulders and squeezed him. "Merlie, you wanna do it?"

The brother nodded.

Early fired his pointer finger at them. "Then we've gotta shake a leg. We've got less than twenty minutes to get you to an airplane. Doc, you get the boys in their coats. Nadine, pack some food they can take."

The brothers scrambled off the bench and, with Grafton pushing them along, hurried away into the front room. Nadine Estes, though, latched onto Early's arm. "You sure you want to do this?"

"Yeah."

"But it'd be awful nice to have those tykes here tonight and tomorrow. Been a long time since Walter and me have had little boys in the house at Christmas."

"I know, but, Nadine, it's right that they be with their sister and her family. They're blood. Come on, box up the cookies. Do that at least."

Early didn't wait for a response. He dashed for the front room where he hauled on his boots, shagged himself into his sheepskin coat, grabbed his hat, and ran for the Jeep, startling Archie when he burst out of the front door.

The dog jumped up. He swung back when the boys and Grafton came hustling out, bundled for the cold. Archie fell in beside them. He trotted along, his ears up, expecting.

Early helped Arland up and into the backseat, then Merlie.

Missus Estes came along behind. She pushed in and held out a five-pound coffee can to Arland. "No coffee in this, Arland. It's cleaned and washed and filled with Christmas cookies, enough that I want you to share with everyone on that airplane and your sister and her family when you get to Texas."

He took the can and hugged it to his chest.

She touched his cheek. "I'm gonna miss you, boy, and Merlie, too. Safe trip now, you hear?"

When she pulled away, Grafton, toting the boys' pillowcase of clothes, stuffed himself into the buddy seat.

Early came in the other side. He fired up the engine and drove the Jeep out, shifting up through second to the road gear when he got away from the buildings. Early held tight to the steering wheel as the Jeep hurtled along toward the county road and highway running down to Seventy-Seven.

BEYOND RILEY, Early slowed. He motioned ahead and off to the side. "Doc, look at that. Henry's a man of his word."

Two command cars—Jeeps with lights flashing and whip antennas flailing the air—burst out of the brush in a far field with two Sherman tanks thundering behind them. The four vehicles fanned out into an attack line and roared on through a snow-filled meadow that separated the military reservation from the civilian world. They flattened a fence, bolted through a ditch, and, as a unit, wheeled right and up onto the highway—a convoy.

Grafton stared across at Early. "Tanks?"

"Henry said we needed big bruisers to block off the highway. Nothing bigger than M-Fours."

Early idled back as he rolled up behind the Tail-end Charlie command car. He held what was for him a new and amazingly slow speed, thirty miles an hour, which for the tank drivers was flat-out racing. Two miles on, the convoy wheeled left onto Highway Seventy-Seven. Beyond the curve, the trailing tank stopped, Tail-end Charlie behind it, and Early, too.

Early bailed out. He ran to the command car while the tank swivelled in place until its bulk laid across both traffic lanes.

Early found the door of the command car open and the driver listening to a transmission on his radio, ". . . ten north of you out of five-thousand, coming down Seventy-Seven. You should be able to see us."

The driver stepped out of his Jeep, his microphone in hand. He jabbed Early and pointed ahead, just above the horizon.

Early shaded his eyes. He saw movement and gave a thumbs-up.

The driver pressed his transmit button. "Gotcha, MATS Six-Seven-One. No wind. You can land either to the south or the north, your choice."

"Will land to the north."

"Roger that." The driver parked his forearm on Early's shoulder. "Man, you've got some pull."

"What I've got is two little boys who want to be with their sister and her husband. He's one of you."

"That's what the colonel said when he got me up on the radio."

"What kind of plane is Six-Seven-One?"

"A Skytrain, a C-Forty-Seven in military parlance. You probably know it as a DC-Three. This one's a medivac flight hauling wounded from Korea. When he passes over us, you skedaddle after him 'cause once the pilot stops, he gonna wait only long enough for you to catch up and get those kids aboard. If that takes more than a couple minutes, he's already said he's outta here."

Early felt the throbbing of the approaching Skytrain's engines. He watched the aircraft winging along off to the left, sliding out of the sky, dipping into a sweeping turn that would bring it around onto a northbound course for landing.

"Ever want to be up there?" Early asked.

"Not for all the gold in Fort Knox."

"Why's that?"

"If I fall, I want to fall no further than from my bed to the floor. I don't even like getting up on a stepladder to change a light bulb. Too high for me."

The throbbing changed to a thrum as the air transport passed overhead, flaps out, its tailwheel skimming the tank's turret.

The driver took a swipe at Early. "Man, get outta here. Get after it."

Early ran back to his Jeep. He clambered in behind the steering wheel. As he settled, he glanced up in his mirror. "Boys, hang on, this is gonna be a wild ride."

Arland, clutching the can of cookies, slid closer to his brother.

Early floored the accelerator. He ripped the Jeep around the command car and onto the shoulder of the highway for a fast run past the butt end of the tank. When clear, he jerked the Jeep back up onto the macadam. Early shifted up into third gear and raced on after the Skytrain slowing, snow billowing out behind it, swirling, snow kicked up by the wash from the aircraft's propellers. The transport rolled to a stop a quarter-mile ahead. Early saw a door open out at the top and arc down, the airstairs visible. He slowed, skirted the aircraft's tail section, and stopped hard beside the door.

Once out, Early yanked his seat forward. He reached for Merlie, caught him under the arms, and lifted him out. Arland came scrambling after, the can of cookies squeezed against his chest.

Grafton, also out, hustled around to the airplane's door where he handed up the stuffed pillowcase to a nurse in a tan jumpsuit waiting there. She moved away, inside, and someone new stepped into the doorway, someone with a white beard, in a red coat and stocking cap and camouflage trousers.

Merlie stared up at him. After a moment, he mouthed the words 'Santa Claus.' He tugged on his brother's sleeve and pointed and repeated this time aloud, "Santa Claus. Look, it's Santa Claus."

Grafton bumped shoulders with Early. "Cactus, I want to know how you got him here."

Note: I wrote this story in December of 2017, the story to be read during the children's service on Christmas Eve morning at the church Marge and I attend. While the target audience was children, I knew well that the adults would be listening, too.

A Child's Christmas

"PAPA, can we go to church tonight?" the girl asked as she and her father walked along, he burdened by a load of firewood he carried on his back.

The girl? Aria Rodriguez, age eight, living in a cave because a hurricane had blown away her home . . . living in a cave with her parents and her baby brother Luis.

What little light that was left in Aria's father's face dimmed. "Ari," he said, "you know the storm destroyed our church, just like it did everything else in our village."

"But the walls are still standing. Father Bernardo showed me."

"They could fall, Ari. It is dangerous."

"Papa, it is the night for the Jesus child. Father Bernardo said so. We should be there."

Aria's father found a large rock. He laid his load aside and sat down. After a moment's rest, he lifted Aria onto his lap. He hugged her. "Ari, we would be the only ones there. You know we have buried many of our neighbors. And those few who survived, they have left. They have gone down the mountain, hoping somewhere to find food and water and someone to help them."

"But we haven't left, Papa."

"No. No, Ari, we have our plot of land, our garden. We have our cow and she has grass in the meadow, so she can survive. And yesterday, yesterday, Ari—" Jose Rodriguez's eyes brightened. "—yesterday I found a spring at the edge of our meadow where we never had a spring before. God's gift perhaps. I cleaned it out and lined it with stones, to keep the water clean for you and me and Momma and little Luis and our cow."

Aria looked up into her father's face. She let her fingers play over his massive hands, gnarled and scarred from working the soil and cutting wood in the forest. "Father Bernardo says we are blessed. Are we?"

"Father Bernardo says that to everyone, Ari. But maybe we are. Our garden, Ari, we have our root crops. And our seed, it is safe in the cave, so we can replant, grow a new garden, grow new crops of corn and melons and beans. Our neighbors, they didn't have a cave, so they lost everything."

Aria cast her gaze down at the straps on her sandals. "I miss Ettien."

"I miss him, too, and his momma and papa and all their children. But Ettein's papa told me they had to go down the mountain. He thought maybe he could find work helping rebuild if they could get to Arecibo. Maybe one day they will come back."

A mongrel dog, tan from the tip of his tail to just shy of his black nose, ventured into the meadow, hesitant. When the dog saw Aria and her father, he broke into a run, whipping his tail as he came, grinning with his lips turned up. The dog slid to a stop at Aria's father's feet, wiggling all over.

Aria slipped down. She hugged the dog. "It's Dario," she said. "It's Ettein's dog. Can we keep him?"

"No, Ari. It would be one more mouth to feed."

"But he hunts. Ettein said so."

"Hmm, perhaps that could be useful, Ari. If anything survived in the forest, it is the wild pigs. We could hunt them for their meat. What we didn't eat would be Dario's." He riffled his fingers through Aria's hair. "Ari, you may keep the dog."

"Thank you, Papa."

"But you will have to explain this to your momma. She does not like dogs."

Aria jerked her face up, surprised. "Is that why we never had a dog?"

Her father nodded. "Come, we must get home," he said as he stood and re-shouldered his burden of firewood.

———————

WHEN THEY neared the cave, Dario the dog bristled. He let out a bark. Just one.

Aria turned in the direction the dog stared. "Papa, there's a man over there by what's left of Ettein's house."

"Yes, I see him."

"He looks hurt. Maybe we should help him."

"I don't know, Ari. He is a stranger."

"But Father Bernardo says—"

Jose Rodriquez frowned. "Ari, with you it's always Father Bernardo says this, Father Bernardo says that." He slung his load of firewood down and took out one stick that he handled like a club. "Just in case," he said and moved out for the rubble that had once been a house and the man poking through it, as if he were searching for something. Ari and the dog hurried to catch up.

"Hey, there," Jose Rodriguez called out. "Can my daughter and me help you?"

The man, dressed in little more than rags, his arm in a sling, looked up. At the sight of Jose Rodriguez's club, he staggered back, tripped and fell among the rubble. "Please, sir," he said, his voice weak, hardly more than a whisper, "I was just looking for something to eat. I meant no harm."

Jose Rodriguez threw his stick aside. "Where are you from?"

"The other side of the mountain. My village was all destroyed. I have been with the dead. The way out was blocked, so I came here."

"How long?"

"Three days."

Aria's father motioned for her to come with him. Together, they helped the man stand. "We salvaged what little food we could find from the houses of the dead in our village, added it to our own supply. My daughter would be disappointed if we did not share."

The man, thin as a reed, gazed down at Aria beside him. His haggard face softened. "Bless you," he whispered.

"Maybe after supper," Aria said, "you could come to church with us. It's the night for the Jesus child."

"The Jesus child, yes, I'd like that."

ARIA, swinging a flashlight and with Dario beside her, ran ahead of her father and her mother carrying little Luis, and the stranger limping along with them. She ran across the village square swept free of debris by the storm that had devastated everything else, ran to the church where Father Bernardo stood in the doorway waiting for anyone who might come. "Father Bernardo," she called out, "we've brought a friend with us."

"Thank you, Ari." He came down the steps, his arms opened out in greeting. "It is so good to see you, Jose and Maria and little Luis." He touched the baby's forehead, and the baby grinned at him.

Father Bernardo looked over at the stranger. "And who do we have here coming to our humble little church tonight?"

"His name is Cristo," Jose Rodriquez said, "from the village of San Mateo. The only survivor."

Father Bernardo smiled. "Like us, yes. God does looks out for us, doesn't He? Come. Come inside." He helped Cristo up the steps and down the aisle to the front bench. "Since there are so few of us, we may as well all be together."

The stranger sat down and the Rodriguez family with him. Maria Rodriguez said something to Aria.

Aria set her flashlight on its base on the bench, the flashlight's beam shooting up into the night's sky. She took baby Luis from her mother and rocked him in her lap.

Father Bernardo, his back to the altar, a lone candle burning there, faced his tiny congregation. He raised his hands. "I cannot but believe that God is looking down upon us, pleased that we have come to His house on this the night of the Jesus child."

He turned to the cradle beside him meant to be a manger for a Nativity. "The doll that has been our Jesus child for so many years, it is lost somewhere. Maria, perhaps you would loan us little Luis?"

She motioned for Aria to take the baby to Father Bernardo. He accepted the child and knelt and laid him in the cradle.

At that moment, a brilliant light shone down from the sky, illuminating the cradle and everything around it.

"The Christmas star," Father Bernardo said, his voice barely audible. "The Christmas star."

That was followed by a whup-whup-whup-whup and the light moving to the side and disappearing.

Outside in the square, a swirl of wind and dust swept up and through the door, flickering the candle whose flame Father Bernardo protected, as Aria protected the baby Luis.

Then silence.

Before Father Bernardo or anyone else could gather their words for what they wanted to say, a man in blue coveralls, a flashlight in one hand and a medic's bag in the other, dashed into the church, followed by a woman dressed as he was.

"We saw your lights," the man said. "We were flying back to Arecibo, looking for survivors on our way. Can we help you?"

Jose Rodriguez rose and gestured toward the stranger. "We have this man—"

But no one sat where the stranger once did. Only a piece of paper held by a flat stone on one corner, the paper fluttering there on the bench as if it were alive.

Aria went to it. She pulled the paper free and handed it to Father Bernardo as he came to her.

The scrawl on the paper glowed iridescent. " 'In as much as you have done it to the least of God's children,' " Father Bernardo read aloud, " 'the lost, the hungry, the injured, you have done it unto me. My blessings to you.' "

Aria peered at the note. "And he signed it."

"Yes," Father Bernardo said as he put his arm around Aria's shoulders. "He signed it Cristo, the Everyman."

Note: Most of the Christmas stories that authors and scriptwriters write are sickly sweet, the stuff of movies for The Hallmark Channel. After having ginned out twenty-five Christmas stories over the years, I thought I had gone dry, that I had shot through every idea that interested me. If I was to write number twenty-six, I had to find a new area to explore. And I found it. The homeless.

One Alone

HE STOOD shivering in the bus shelter, he in his mack with the hoodie pulled up, camo cargo pants and boots, waiting for the Nine-Twenty, the last bus running from the mall to downtown. With nothing to do other than try to keep warm, he peered up at the snowflakes dancing and twirling their way down through a yellowish cone of light from a nearby street lamp, mesmerized by nature's ballet.

A car rolled by, splashing slush, soaking his pant legs. He jumped back, too late. Surely some fool in a hurry to get to the Culver's up the street for a flavor of the day before the restaurant's closing time, he thought.

A horn blatted.

He turned toward the sound, a set of headlights coming his way, the headlights of a big honker of a vehicle—the Big Blue People Shaker.

The Shaker slowed as it sidled up to the shelter, air hissing out of the bus's leveler, lowering the front of the vehicle several inches most particularly for the handicapped and the elderly.

The door opened and hot air whooshed out, the air smelling of diesel fumes and an overworked heater.

The driver, a hefty woman in a fur-collared jacket and JVL Transit ball cap, waved him aboard. "Sorry to be runnin' late, Andy. Hope you not been waitin' long."

Andreo 'Andy' Delio dropped his dollar in the chute that carried the fare down to a toll box beneath the floor. "Just a couple minutes, Babe. Only warmed my anticipation for seeing you."

"Bet you say dat to all us women drivers."

He smiled, a tired smile, and drifted back to a seat on the starboard side. Further back—all the way back—a trio of teen girls, surrounded by packages, tapped away at their cells' screens while gabbing together and giggling. Forward of him sat an old couple, on the port side, clutching Christmas shopping bags on their laps, both stone-faced silent.

The Shaker started up, so Delio settled in to sleep, knowing the driver would wake him before his stop.

But several minutes in, The Shaker slowed, then halted—an unscheduled stop. He sensed it and nudged up an eyelid in time to see two guys coming up the steps, both in hoodies—black, not brown like his. The one in front brought a pistol out from his waistband. He shoved it in the driver's face.

"Gimme yer money now," he said.

The driver stared at him. "What kinda fool you are, funderbutt? Look down dere—" She tipped her head toward the chute. "—da fare money's in a locked box unner da floor. I cain't get it, an' you cain't either."

"Yer own money, then, old lady."

"Well, now, you jus' hep yourself. Wallet's on da dash. All dat's in it is my CDL."

"No dead presidents? No plastic?"

"Huh-uh."

"Yer watch and cell, then."

"Don't have neither, not on my paycheck."

"Bitch." He wheeled on his partner and thrust him down the aisle. "Get theirs. Clean 'em out."

The partner dug out his own gun as he neared the old couple.

Delio decided he'd had enough, so he let his one open eye close and his chin dip down until it rested on his chest. He started counting the seconds. At twenty-four, he felt a gun barrel prod his shoulder.

"Yo, you. I want yer stuff."

A second prod came. And a third.

"Hey, I think dis guy's dead."

Delio sensed the wannabe bad boy had looked away. With the quickness of a snake striking, he grabbed the front of the man's sweatshirt and yanked him down, rammed his head into the wall, leaving him in a heap. Delio snatched up the man's gun and rolled out into the aisle. He trained the pistol on the first robber. "Buddy," he said, his voice a poor imitation of Clint Eastwood, "I've been in two wars. I'm a dead shot. You sure you wanna go against me?"

"To hell wich you!"

The robber tensed.

Delio saw it, knew what was next and jacked off the first shot, the bullet smashing through the man's gun hand and ripping up his arm before he could feel the searing pain and react.

Delio raced forward. He threw the robber on the floor. "Babe, whatcha got I can tie him with?"

She thrust a scarf into his hand, and he bound the robber's hands behind his back, one of the hands bloody, the robber yelping.

Delio slapped him in the back of the head. "Dumb ass. You're lucky you're not dead." He glanced up at the teens in the back. "Call nine-one-one."

Delio, done with his tying chores, rolled away to the driver. "Babe, I've never been here. I don't need the attention. You don't know me or my name."

He scrambled down the steps. Outside, in the snow, he ran to a curbside trash can. There he wiped the gun free of fingerprints and threw it in. When Delio had the driver's eye, he motioned at the trash can and trotted off into the gloom, the wail of a police siren—music of the night—coming from the direction of the city center.

"KINDA LATE, aren'tcha?" the man on the door said as he stepped aside for Delio.

Delio pushed his way on in. He stopped under the glow of an overhead light and stamped the snow from his boots. "Bud, it's not a half-bad night out there."

"Hell, man, it's snowing."

"Not that much, so I went for a walk on the river trail. It's quiet."

"Yup, well, I guess quiet's good for the soul. Hey, there was a robbery and shootout on a city bus tonight. Heard it on the police scanner. You know about that?"

Delio shrugged.

"Well, anyway I kept your room for ya. Here's the key."

The key was a card with a magnetic strip on it, making the rooms at The Homeless Hilton, as Delio called the place, more secure than if they had key locks on the doors.

He took the card and went on upstairs. There he flopped his butt down on his bed and shucked himself out of his mack. Delio saw something—a hole in the side of his coat and a second, an entrance and an exit. He fingered them, wondered about them.

He'd heard only one shot—his, he thought.

He raised his shirt and touched his fingers to his side.

DELIO SAT on a bench in the mall employees' locker room, tucking the cuffs of his Santa pants into the tops of his boots.

His supervisor came swinging around the corner, a white beard in his hand. "Deal, how long you been here?"

Delio kept tucking. "Three weeks."

"In that time you sure haven't said much about yourself."

"Not much to say."

The supervisor held up the beard. "I had the girls in our beauty salon wash and style it for you. Looks pretty good, don't you think?"

Delio took the beard and hooked the loops over his ears. He adjusted the elastic until he had a tight fit, then put on his square Santa glasses and checked himself in the mirror behind the supervisor. "Bobby, thanks for this. You're a good man, no matter what the others say."

"What?"

"Nothing."

The supervisor took Delio's place on the bench. He parked his elbows on his knees and watched his Santa pull on his fur-edged red jacket. "Your line-'em-up elf, she's gotta quit tonight. Know anyone we could get on short notice to take her place?"

Delio peered in the mirror at the supervisor. "I might."

"Can you get her in here before your shift starts tomorrow afternoon?"

"Probably."

"Probably's not good enough."

"All right, she's not working anywhere else, so, yes."

"Deal, I'll see that you get a finder's fee if she turns out to be any good."

"How much?"

"Twenty-five bucks."

"Make it thirty." He put on his wig and his Santa hat, shifting the hat to the side until he had it at a jaunty angle. "So Viv's quitting. How come?"

"Oh, her husband's taken a turn for the worst. She says she's gotta be home with him. You know how these things happen."

"Yeah, life has a way of busting in. Bobby, I've gotta get out on the throne. Children will be waiting for jolly old Saint Nick."

"Uh-huh. By the way, how old are you, Nick? You didn't list your birthday on your job app."

"Federal regs. You and the mall can't ask me that. But I'm fifty-six."

The supervisor raked his fingers up the sides of his head and through his hair, fluffing out his mane. "My dad tells me that's a good age. I guess I'll find out in another twenty-eight years."

"Yup, Bobby, you're still a kid. If you're nice to the end of the season, on my last day I'll let you sit on Santa's lap, even let the photo elf take a picture of you and me."

DELIO RAPPED on the door of The Homeless Hilton's room two-thirteen, the light above him flickering. It ffsssted and went out.

Delio, still in his mack, rapped again. "Alice, you in there?"

He heard slippers slapping across the tile floor toward the door, that followed by the sound of a deadbolt sliding.

The door opened a couple inches revealing a chain latch still in place, a TV illuminating the inside of the room. An eye appeared above the chain.

Delio pushed his hoodie back off his head. "Alice, you all right?"

"Just watchin' Skin Wars on the Game Channel."

"Skin Wars?"

"Body painting, Deal. Third season for the show. The winner gets a hundred thou."

"Sweetie, it's not gonna be you or me. You gonna let me in?"

She unlatched the chain and opened the door.

The room, stuffy, gave off the air of stale cigarette smoke. The Homeless Hilton was, by city regulation, smoke-free and booze-free. A violation of either could get a resident bounced to the curb.

Delio gandered around.

"I smoke outside," Alice Ferrell said. "It gets on my clothes."

"So the smell comes inside with you. All right, are you sober?"

"You're damn direct."

"Well, are you?"

She shuffled back into the kitchenette. "I've not had a beer in a week, and I go to my meetings."

He peered at her, at her back. "How're you doing for money?"

"The truth?"

"The truth."

She twisted around and leaned against the counter. "Well, I'm a couple feet shy of desperate."

"Your disability check?"

"It's late. Again. You wanna sit down?"

Delio helped himself to a folding chair at the card table that served as the kitchenette's table. In a corner on a rolling stand, a tall blonde on the TV's screen introduced a new contestant.

Ferrell turned the set off. She went to the hot plate for the coffeepot. This she held out to Delio. "Want some?"

"Still making your famous Navy coffee?"

"Thick enough to cut."

"Then slice me off a half a cup."

Ferrell partially filled a hard-used, grungy Melmac cup and topped off a second. The partially filled she set in front of Delio.

He gazed at its blackness. "Is this the real stuff or decaf?"

She laughed, laughed hard, and took the folding chair opposite Delio.

"Alice, I've got a job for you, and you can't say no."

"I FEEL SILLY," she said as she curtsied in her elf's costume before Delio, he in his Santa togs and beard.

"Ho-ho-ho, get over it," he said in his best Santa voice. "The money's good. Now let's go over this one last time."

Alice Ferrell fished in the bag on her belt. She brought out a pad of sticky notes and a pen. "I patrol the line of waiting kids and parents, and I talk to them and tell them they won't have to wait long."

"And when you see I'm about finished with the child on my lap?"

"I go to the first kid in the line and get his or her name from the parent. I write it on a Post-It to give to the photo elf, then I bring the kid to you and I say, 'Santa, this is' and I give you the kid's name, and I tell you he or she's been good this year and go back to patrolling the line."

"See? It's easy."

"If you like kids, but, dammit, Deal, I hate kids."

"Not today you don't."

He took her by the elbow and guided her down the hall toward the entrance to Santa Land, but she broke away. "I forgot my coffee. Be back in a sec."

ELF ALICE took a nod from Santa and hurried to the head of the line of anxious children and concerned parents. "And your kid's name is?" she asked the first mother.

"John Smith."

"It's been a long afternoon, ma'am. Really? John Smith?"

The boy, a CPA look-alike in a suit and tie, his necktie askew, puffed himself up. "I am the real John Smith," he said, "and I'm nine years old."

She wrote his name on her pad. "All right, Johnny."

"John. I'm John Smith."

She rubbed her forehead above one eye, squinting. "Yes, John. John Smith. Let me take you to Santa. He's just about ready for you."

Together, they marched to the throne where Santa sent a little girl on her way clutching a candy cane.

Santa gazed up at his elf. "And who do we have here?"

The boy squared himself up Army-straight. "You don't remember me? I was here last year. And the year before. I thought you knew every child."

Elf Alice palmed her sticky note into Santa's gloved hand. He glanced at the note. "Sometimes I forget, but you I do remember." He palmed the note back and put his hands on the boy's shoulders. "You're John Smith."

"The real John Smith," the boy said.

"Yes, so you told me last year and the year before, the real John Smith. Would you like to sit on Santa's lap and have your picture taken with me?"

"I'm too old to sit on your lap, but I'll stand beside you."

Santa moved the boy around to his side. He put his arm around the boy's shoulders and pointed to a camera attached to a screen and a computer, the photo elf, a string bean of a woman, at the ready.

She banged off a picture. "How about another?" she asked. "And in this one, Santa, would you tilt your head toward the boy—"

"John Smith," the boy announced.

"Yes, toward Master Smith. That's it." She shot a second photo and, after she looked at the image on her screen, waved an okay.

Santa drew the boy closer. "Tell me, John Smith, what do you want for Christmas?"

The boy brought out an iPhone. "I've made a list. I have it right here."

He tapped the screen.

Elf Alice slipped away, behind the throne, and sucked in a swallow from her Starbuck's cup.

SANTA HELD a whimpering child out to Elf Alice. "Got a leaker here. Take her back to her mother and get me a towel before you bring the next kid up."

THE PHOTO ELF placed a card on a tripod near the head of the waiting line, the card announcing SANTA MUST FEED HIS REINDEER. HE'LL BE BACK IN 10 MINUTES.

"Really?" one mother asked. "We've already been waiting ten minutes."

The elf eased in close to the questioner. "The truth is Santa has a bladder problem. He has to go to the bathroom."

The mother looked down at her three small ones. "I guess we can wait a little longer, can't we?"

"Mommy, do we have to?" one asked.

The elf hurried away to Santa coming down from his throne. "If I had told them this was your coffee break, they would have rioted. So I told them you had to hit the head."

"They bought it?"

"Yes, they did."

"Elf Connie, you are true to your name. You're an A-number-one con."

They went around the throne, toward the exit door, but Delio stopped when he saw his line-'em-up elf behind the throne, tossing back a swallow from her Starbuck's. He snatched her cup away. "Alice, you're slurring your words. What have you got in here?"

He peered into the cup, the contents—what little that was left—clear, not black. "Vodka?" he asked.

She gave off a pitiful look, like a dog that had been whipped. "I needed a bracer to get me through."

"Bracer, hell. Alice, you're going home sick. If Bobby had caught you, he'd have fired your fanny. And when you get home, call your sponsor."

"But, Deal—"

"The only butt here is yours. Get it back in the program. Connie will cover for you the rest of the night."

DELIO BANGED on the door of two-thirteen. "Alice, you in there?"

When no response came, he hauled the Homeless Hilton's night manager forward, the night manager clutching a key card. He slid it into the slot beneath the door's handle.

The lock clicked, and the night manager pushed the door open.

"Alice!" Delio called out as he barged in. He gazed around the room, the room as disheveled as he had often seen its occupant. "Damn, she's not here. Bud, I need to use your office phone to call the police."

The night manager threw up his hands. "Waste o' time, man. She's a drunk. They're not gonna do nuthin'."

"Maybe, maybe not. I still need to use your phone." Delio turned. He hustled out of the room and down the stairs to the office, the door open and the night manager behind him.

Delio helped himself to the desk phone. After he consulted a card he took from his shirt pocket, he punched in a string of numbers and waited, eying the night manager. "You got a number for her sponsor?"

"I've got the numbers for all the sponsors of our guests."

"I want you to call Alice's sponsor. Find out if she's been in contact."

The night manager went around to his side of the desk and pulled out a drawer.

"Yeah?" came a voice through the telephone's receiver.

Delio pressed the handset to his ear. "Morry? It's Deal. One of the Hilton's residents has disappeared. I need your help."

"With what?"

"Finding her."

"Deal, my cell says it's ten-fifteen. She'll come home when the bars close."

"Morry, this is important."

"How important?"

"I've got the feeling life-and-death important."

"All right, how long's she been missing?"

"Three hours."

"That's it? Deal, we don't do anything until someone's been missing for twenty-four."

"Morry, she's A.A. You're A.A."

Silence.

Delio fiddled with the police detective's business card while he waited for Morry Gilman to say something.

The something came in the form of Gilman clearing his throat.

"Well?" Delio asked.

"Pick you up in ten."

A MAN STAGGERED out of the Company B Firehouse Bar, his coat misbuttoned and his cap screwed on half to the side. He plowed into Delio and Gilman coming up the snow-dusted walk. "S'cuse me," he mumbled. "Needa bum a ride. I'm too inebe, too inebe–too sloshed to drive."

Gilman flashed his badge.

The drunk stumbled back a step.

Gilman brought out his cell. He tapped open the jail's mug shot of Alice Ferrell and held it up to the drunk. "You see this woman tonight?"

"She in trouble?"

"No, she won the lottery. Have you seen her?"

"Not that I kin 'member. Need a ride. Kin I get one?"

Gilman glanced up at a police cruiser coming his way. He waved it over and opened the back passenger door. "In," he said, aiming the drunk inside. "Watch it. Don't clonk your head."

He hooked the man into a seat belt and shoulder harness and, while he did, talked out of the corner of his mouth to the patrolman behind the wheel. "Take this guy home, Tommy, and, if he can't get in or hasn't got a home, take him to jail and let him sleep it off."

"Right, Detective. Want me to write him up?"

"Oh, come on, it's almost Christmas. Show a little love."

"The night sergeant won't like it."

"You tell him for me tough tiddlywinks." Gilman closed the door. He slapped the roof twice, and the cruiser rolled away.

Delio clapped the detective on the shoulder. "Tough tiddlywinks?"

"What, you want I should say tough horse pucky?"

"Let him sleep it off? Don't ticket him? Gilly, you've got a heart of mush."

"Don't let the word get around."

They went on inside, a Christmas show running on the TV over the bar and nobody watching it. Delio looked up at the television. "That show, you know that one?"

Gilman glanced up. "Can't say as I do."

"It's a Jimmy Stewart special, *Mr. Krueger's Christmas.*" He pointed. "See there, there's Stewart. He's playing Mister Krueger, a janitor, and right there he's directing the Mormon Tabernacle Choir. This was filmed back in Nineteen Seventy-nine."

"What, you're a television historian now?"

Delio hooked a thumb in his coat pocket. "Better. I was in it."

"The heck you say."

The bartender, built like a pro wrestler, sidled up. He slapped a Company B coaster in front of Delio and one in front of Gilman. "What'll it be, fellas?"

Gilman flipped out his badge and brought his cell's screen up next to it. "This woman, has she been in here tonight?"

The bartender leaned down on his elbows and studied the picture. "Alice. Yes, Alice Ferrell. No, 'fraid not. The last time she was in here was a couple weeks ago."

"What was she drinking?"

"Beer. That cheap stuff from Monroe. Said she was at the end of her disability check." The bartender scooped a pilsner glass out of the wash sink beneath the bar. He stripped the water off the glass and polished it dry with a towel. "Why you looking for her?"

"She's missing."

"Hmm." The bartender set the pilsner away with the other clean glasses on the back bar. From there, he reached up for the fire bell mounted next to the TV and rang the bell three times. A half-dozen heads turned toward him. "Anyone here know Alice Ferrell?"

One hand went up.

"You seen her anywhere tonight? I've got a cop here says she's missing."

The man shook his head and went back to his Jack and Coke.

The bartender planted his hands on the bar in front of Gilman. "Sorry. You want me to call around to some of our other places of refreshment?"

"We've been to all of them in the downtown. Yours is the last."

"Well, I'll still call around. Badges and police uniforms don't always inspire truthfulness among the people in my trade."

Gilman handed his business card across. "Call me if you find out anything."

DELIO AND GILMAN stepped back out into the snow, the wind having come up. Gilman turned up his collar. "Look, I'll send an alert along with Alice's photo to the computer in ever police car we've got. That'll get us more eyes on the street, so maybe someone'll see her."

Delio hunched up in his mack, his hoodie pulled down to his eyebrows. "You know, maybe the judge ought to order all us alkies and geek monsters to have one of those chip things embedded under the skin on our arm. That way we could ping someone who goes missing."

"That's a sci-fi world," Gilman said as the two stepped along toward The Homeless Hilton a block away. "So, tell me, if I can find *Mr. Krueger's Christmas* on Netflix, how will I know you? Which scenes are you in?"

"Only one. I'm the skinny guy playing second trumpet in the Salvation Army band."

"You get Jimmy Stewart's autograph?"

Delio rummaged in an inside pocket for his wallet. He found it, brought it out, and, from an inside cavity, brought out a folded paper, the paper worn at the folds, the folds creases. This paper he passed to Gilman.

Gilman opened it. The cover page from a script, the title there—*Mr. Krueger's Christmas*—and the name of the screenwriter on the top half. Scrawled across the bottom half, *Young Mr. Delio, you sure swing on the brass. With respect, your newest best friend, James Stewart. Merry Christmas!*

Gilman refolded the page. "They're not gonna believe this down at the cop shop."

Delio clamped onto Gilman's arm. He hauled him to a stop. "No, this you don't tell to anybody."

"Why not? Deal, what are you hiding from?"

DELIO'S SUPERVISOR, sweat beading out on his forehead, grabbed him at the door to Santa Land. "Where's you line-'em-up elf? Where's Alice what's-her-name?"

"I don't know. She wasn't in her room when I left for work."

"And you weren't going to tell me?"

"Connie's going to cover for her, Bobby. She can do both jobs."

"Not well."

"Well enough. Really well if you give her her pay and Alice's pay, both."

The supervisor twisted away. He paced. "Deal, are you trying to rob me?"

"I'm just trying to get through to Christmas." Delio waggled two white-gloved fingers. "Two more days and we've got it done, man."

The supervisor scratched at the five o'clock shadow on the side of his face. "You really think Connie can do both?"

"Absolutely. We've got it worked out. Tell her she gets double pay for these last two days."

Delio fluffed up his stomach padding and went on out into Santa Land. As he took his seat on the throne, Elf Connie hustled in from the locker room, hustled up to him. "Bobby's gonna give me double pay for doin' my job and Alice's job. Did you have anything to do with this?"

"Ho, ho, no!"

DELIO RAPPED on the manager's door at the Homeless Hilton.

A woman's voice responded with "Come."

Delio opened the door.

The manager, Maria Razzota by the name plate on her desk, motioned him in. She leaned back in her chair. "Andy, how can I help you?"

"Maybe I can help you."

"How's that?"

He threw his leg across an armless side chair and sat down. "I've come into some money."

"Does that mean you're going to be leaving us?"

"And take on the hassle of renting an apartment, maybe having to find someone to share it with?" Delio gave a quick shake of his head. "No, I want to give you the money."

"For the Hilton?"

"And for the things this place does for people like me."

She leaned on her elbow on the arm of the chair as he brought out a wad of twenty-dollar bills, a thumb going under her chin and a forefinger up beside her face.

He counted out the money on the desk—seven hundred forty dollars. Delio pushed it to Razzota. "I want you to do two things with this. Divvy up two-thirds with the residents and take them on a shopping trip to the mall. Do it tomorrow."

"The day before Christmas? Andy, what a treat. And the rest?"

"On Christmas Day, take everybody out to dinner."

"Can I tell them who's buying?"

"Just say it's an anonymous donor. All the time you're getting anonymous donations."

"That's how we keep the doors open." Razzota held a bill up to her desk lamp. "This isn't funny money, is it?"

"It's real. All new bills I picked up this morning at the Fifth National. Call the bank president if you want. He'll confirm it."

"So how did you—"

"I'm Santa Claus. Well, at the mall, at least. But you can't tell anyone that, either."

"Of course. Nobody sees behind the beard." Razzota squared up the stack of bills. "Andy, you've been with us for almost a year. In all that time, I've never been able to figure you out."

"Isn't it nice to have a little mystery in your life?"

THE BIG BLUE People Shaker rolled up to the stop at the mall. Maria Razzota swung out of the first seat and raised her hand for the passengers' attention. "All right, everybody, you've got an hour to shop. At five o'clock, you meet me at Santa Land. We're going to take a group picture with Santa, then we're going to supper at Culver's, all right?"

Scattered applause came from the passengers on the bus. They rose en masse and shuffled out into the aisle, working their way forward.

Razzota, now at the bottom of the steps, counted her charges as they passed by—thirty-seven with the last, Herbie Stein, a brain-injured vet hobbling down to the curb on two canes. "Herbie, you okay?" she asked after she checked him off.

"Fine, just not gonna win any races. As usual." He went on, trailing the others.

Razzota stepped back into The Shaker. She waved up to the driver. "Babe, you'll pick us up at five-thirty?"

"Count on it, sweetheart."

"I can see why Andy Delio likes you so much."

"You know Deal? Ain't he sumthin'? If I wasn't so well married, I'd get that fella for myself."

"AND I WANT a Play-All-Day Elmo, a Pie Face game, a Party Time Kitchen, a Girl Scout Cookies oven, a Shopkins Bubbleisha, an Exploding Kittens card game," the girl said, running off her list to Santa, Delio only half listening, wondering would she ever reach the end? Then he saw them, residents from The Homeless Hilton filtering into Santa Land, stopping in front of the lollypop fence, talking, laughing, showing off their purchases to one another, Razzota counting the residents against the list on her clipboard.

Herbie Stein slow-cruised up in one of the mall's motorized shopping carts, his canes and Christmas-wrapped packages in the basket.

The girl looked hard at Santa. "Are you listening to me?"

Delio blinked. "Exploding Kittens? Are you sure?"

"We're all playing it, but I don't have my own cards for when my friends come to my house."

"I see. I'll make a note of that, dear." Santa stroked his beard. "But it seems to me that your list is awfully long. With all the other children in the world, you may not get everything. I hope you understand."

She jammed her fist into her waist. "I hope you understand my father's a lawyer."

He, forcing a smile, held up a candy cane.

She snatched it away, pushed off from his lap, and stalked off toward the picture-taking elf, Elf Connie.

Delio's supervisor materialized in front of Delio with Razzota beside him. He motioned back to the residents. "Santa, we have a group of people here who'd like to have their picture taken with you. It would be good publicity for the mall—homeless people given a shopping spree by an unknown benefactor. Whaddaya think?"

Delio gazed over the collection. He waggled a gloved hand at them, waggled for them to come forward. The supervisor went about the business of arranging them around the throne.

Delio beckoned to Stein working his way up, the last of the Hilton's residents. "Want to sit on the arm of my throne next to me?"

Stein responded with a pained grin and continued up one step at a time. When he got up on the throne's platform, he turned and parked himself on the arm, pooching out his cheeks with a great exhale of breath.

Delio put a hand on Stein's leg. "You having a good day, Herbie?"

An eyebrow jutted up. "How do you know my name?"

"I'm Santa Claus. I know everybody's name. Now tell me, what do you want for Christmas that you haven't already gotten for yourself?"

Stein, listing to the side, pushed against one of his canes to straightened himself. "I'd like to see my ma, but that's not possible."

"Where is she?"

"You don't know?"

"Herbie, I have so many details to keep sorted out, sometimes I get confused."

"Waltonville, Illinois. She's in the nursing home there."

"Waltonville. Let me see what my elves and I can do."

Stein rubbed his chin. "Boy, your voice is familiar. Do I know you?"

The supervisor clapped his hands. "All right, everybody, look right here—" He moved over to Elf Connie. "—we're going to take the picture."

She snapped three in rapid succession. She studied them on the screen, made her selection, and waved an okay to the group. As they began to wander in bunches away from the throne, she tapped in thirty-eight and touched PRINT.

A patrolman, in a parka and boots, elbowed his way through and up to Santa Claus. He leaned down. "Santa. Mister Delio, Detective Gilman wants me to bring you to him. We've found someone."

DELIO, BACK in his civilian garb, shoved the passenger door of the cruiser open and stepped out into dust devils of swirling snow. Ahead and down the slope from the street, closer to the river, flood lights illuminated a gathering of people—firemen Delio could see, a paramedic crew, a couple beat cops, and several divers in rubber suits with air tanks on their backs. Gilman, among them, knelt at the side of a rescue basket.

Delio ran down and stopped beside Gilman.

Gilman peered up at him. "Deal, I'm sorry, it's Alice. One of our guys walking the river trail spotted her body floating in an eddy below the dam."

He peeled a blanket back. "I'm thinking she jumped off a bridge upstream of the dam, probably Veterans Memorial. It's pretty high."

Delio's eyes clouded. He twisted away. "But why? Why jump? Why now?"

Gilman laid the blanket back over the face. "God only knows, and He hasn't sent down any messages."

"But Christmas Eve?"

Gilman pushed himself up. As he did, he swatted the snow from the knees of his trousers. "Deal, you're not going to do something stupid, like immerse yourself in a bottle of hooch, are you?"

"No." He looked up at the night sky, at the snow filtering down. "I think I'd like to go to church."

"All right, which one? I'll get you a ride."

"Saint Nicholas."

DELIO WAITED as the crowd from the early mass made their way out of the church and down the snow-covered steps to the street, some talking, a few laughing, others silent, seemingly, by the expressions on their faces, at peace. When the last passed by, Delio made his way up and inside, into the warmth of the narthex, the air rich with incense and the scent of fresh pine greens.

He shoved his hoodie back and stripped off his gloves. At the holy water stoup, Delio dipped his fingers in and crossed himself, then went down the aisle. At the front, he knelt at the communion rail.

Behind him and above—from the choir loft—he heard some several people talking, women—a soprano and an alto—and another someone noodling on the organ, picking out a melody.

He felt a puff of air to his side as a door opened. Someone came in, stopped at the bank of vigil candles Delio figured from the silence, then came on. He felt a hand touch his shoulder.

"Deal, you're late for early mass and early for late mass. Are you all right?"

Delio crossed himself once more. He swivelled around and sat on the kneeling bench. He leaned back against the railing.

The someone—a priest—sat down next to him. Father Roderigo Madrigal, called Father Rod by most. "So," Madrigal said, "what's going on here? Deal, you're not that good a Catholic."

"I'm a Methodist, you know that, trying to learn your way 'cause it's so much more peaceful here."

"Come to bingo some Tuesday night. It's far from peaceful."

"Yeah, maybe. But here . . . and now." He drifted his hand through the air. "A friend killed herself."

Madrigal hugged his knees. "And on Christmas Eve when we celebrate a new life in the world that would change the world." He peered sidewards at Delio. "You're wondering what, why?"

"Yeah."

"She one of the residents at The Hilton?"

"Yeah."

"Have problems?"

"Lots. Lots of demons in her life."

Madrigal let go of his knees. He stretched his legs out in front of him. "Maybe this was her way to peace. Yours was Hillybilly Heroin. Mine was Angel Dust."

"But you got your life right."

Madrigal placed his hand on Delio's knee. "You did, too, my friend."

"With your help."

"With Jesus' help and maybe a bit from me. How did your friend do it?"

"She jumped from a bridge."

Madrigal sucked on his teeth. "Have you thought that maybe Jesus was there and caught her soul before she hit the water?"

"Do you think?"

"I think I prefer to. See, my Jesus is a caring Jesus. So is yours."

"Still and all—"

"No still and all. You gonna stay for our next mass? It's Christmas Eve, Deal."

LEAVE ME A REVIEW!

If you enjoyed this book, please take a moment to leave a review on Amazon. I'm always interested in learning what you like, think and want. I read all the reviews personally.

On Amazon, go to my *Tis the Season* book page, then scroll down to customer reviews.

Thank you for your support!

ACKNOWLEDGMENTS

I've been an indie author for a long time, bringing out my books under my Windstar Press imprint since 2011. My, that's only eight years ago. Perhaps I haven't been an indie author all that long,

We indies, loners that we are, nonetheless depend on a lot of people to make our stories and books the best that they can be. Lance Buckley, a superb cover designer, worked with me on this volume, as he has on several others.

Just as a knock-out cover is vital to grabbing potential readers, so are the words on the back cover that say this book is one you really should buy. For those words, I turned to fellow writer and mentor Marshall Cook. Marshall has more than forty books to his credit, either as author or editor.

I always close with a thank you to all librarians around the country. They, like you and your fellow readers who have enjoyed my James Early mysteries, my AJ Garrison crime novels, my John Wads crime novellas, my Wings Over the Mountains novels, and my short story collections, have been real boosters. Without them and you, there would be no reason to write.

A NOTE FROM THE AUTHOR

The first Christmas story I wrote was a part of a novel, that novel never published. So I pulled the Christmas story out, shaped it up and polished it, then I shared it with family and friends as my Christmas gift to them.

I wrote a new story the next year and the next and the next.

And a tradition was established.

Twenty-six years later, I'm still writing Christmas stories.

You've just read eleven of my very best.

It was my pleasure to share them with you.

Jerry

Janesville, Wisconsin, November 2019

WHAT PEOPLE SAY ABOUT MY BOOKS

Early's Fall, a James Early Mystery, book 1. . . "If James Early were on the screen instead of in a book, no one would leave the room." – Robert W. Walker, author of *Children of Salem*

Early's Winter, a James Early Mystery, book 2 . . . "Jerry Peterson's *Early's Winter* is a fine tale for any season. A little bit Western, a little bit mystery, all add up to a fast-paced, well-written novel that has as much heart as it does darkness. Peterson is a first-rate storyteller. Give *Early's Winter* a try, and I promise you, you'll be begging for the next James Early novel. Spring can't come too soon." – Larry D. Sweazy, Spur-award winning author of *The Badger's Revenge*

The Watch, an AJ Garrison Crime Novel, book 1 . . . "Jerry Peterson has written a terrific mystery, rich in atmosphere of place and time. New lawyer A.J. Garrison is a smart, gutsy heroine." – James Mitchell, author of *Our Lady of the North*

Rage, an AJ Garrison Crime Novel, book 2 . . . "Terrifying. Just–terrifying. Timely and profound and even heartbreaking. Peterson's taut spare style and truly original voice create a high-tension page turner. I really loved this book." – Hank Phillippi Ryan, Agatha, Anthony and Macavity winning author

The Last Good Man, a Wings Over the Mountains novel, Book 1 . . . Jerry Peterson joins the ranks of the writer's writer–that is, an author other authors can learn from, as in how to open and close a book, but also in how to run the course." – Robert W. Walker, author of *Curse of the RMS Titanic*

Capitol Crime, a Wings Over the Mountains novel, Book 2 . . . "In *Capitol Crime*, Peterson's vivid characters jump right off the page, and his sharp detail and snappy dialog puts the reader right in the middle of Prohibition-era action and one of the wildest schemes ever to take down a bootlegging ring. So buckle up. You're in for a hellava ride!" – J. Michael Major, author of *One Man's Castle*

Iced, a John Wads Crime Novella, book 1 . . . "Jerry Peterson's new thriller is a thrill-a-minute ride down a slippery slope of suspense and shootouts. Engaging characters, spiffy dialogue, and non-stop action make this one a real winner." – Michael A. Black, author of *Sleeping Dragons*, a Mack Bolan Executioner novel

Rubbed Out, a John Wads Crime Novella, book 2 . . . "Jerry Peterson's latest thriller gives us, once again, an endearing hero, a townfull of suspects, and quick action leading to a surprising climax. If you like your thrills to be delivered by strong characters in a setting that matters, this one's for you." – Betsy Draine, co-author with Michael Hinden of *Murder in Lascaux* and *The Body in Bodega Bay*

A James Early Christmas and *The Santa Train*, Christmas short story collections . . . "These stories are charming, heart-warming, and well-written. It's rare today to see stories that unabashedly champion simple generosity and good will, but Jerry Peterson does both successfully, all the while keeping you entertained with his gentle humor. This should definitely go under your tree this season." – Libby Hellmann, author of *Nice Girl Does Noir*, a collection of short stories

A James Early Christmas – Book 2, a Christmas short story collection . . . "What brings these Christmas tales to life is the compassion of their protagonist and their vivid sense of time and place. James Early's human warmth tempers the winter landscape of the Kansas plains in the years after World War II. A fine collection." – Michael Hinden, co-author with Betsy Draine of the Nora Barnes and Toby Sandler mysteries

The Cody & Me Chronicles, a Christmas short story collection and more . . . "Jerry Peterson is a fireside tale-spinner, warm and wistful, celebrating what is extraordinary in ordinary people with homespun grace." – John Desjarlais, author of *Specter*

Flint Hills Stories, Stories I Like to Tell – Book 1 . . . "Jerry Peterson's short stories are exactly how short stories should be: quick, but involving; pleasant, but tense; and full of engaging characters and engaging conflicts. I can think of few better ways to spend an afternoon than being submerged in James Early's Kansas." – Sean Patrick Little, author of *The Bride Price*

Smoky Mountain Stories, Stories I Like to Tell – Book 2 . . . "Jerry Peterson's SMOKY MOUNTAIN STORIES is pure Jerry Peterson magic. His years as a journalist have shaved his prose down to a razor's edge, the kind of flinty steel wordplay that only comes from someone who has logged a lifetime at the keyboard." – Sean Patrick Little, author of *After Everyone Died*

Fireside Stories, Stories I Like to Tell – Book 3 . . . "Witty and clever, Jerry Peterson spins a tale with a deft pen and an ear for dialogue that you don't find too often. There's an old-fashioned sense of character and craft in Peterson's works that will have you desperate for more." – Sean Patrick Little, author, *The Bride Price*

A Year of Wonder, Stories I Like to Tell – Book 4 . . . "These 24 short gems run the gamut from humorous to mysterious, including a welcome return of Sheriff James Early. You'll wish that a year had more than 12 months in it so that you could have more of these fine stories! A very good year, indeed."

– Ted Hertel, Jr., recipient of MWA's Robert L. Fish (Edgar) Award for Best First Short Story by an American author

The James Early Reader, Stories I Like to Tell – Book 5 . . . "Jerry Peterson is a master storyteller. *The James Early Reader* is set on the Great Plains of mid-twentieth century Kansas where Peterson weaves rugged, heartfelt magic out of bluestem pastures and stony flint-capped hills. Do yourself a favor and give this book a read." – J.M. Hayes, author of the Mad Dog & Englishman mysteries and *The Spirit and the Skull*

Hyper Fiction: 50 stories for people in a hurry – Book 1 . . . "Witty and clever, Jerry Peterson spins a tale with a deft pen and an ear for dialogue that you don't find too often. There's an old-fashioned sense of character and craft in Peterson's works that will have you desperate for more." – Sean Patrick Little, author of *Lord Bobbins and the Romanian Ruckus*

Hyper Fiction: 50 stories for people in a hurry – Book 2 . . . "You'll find loads to love here, good stories sprinkled with bursts of illumination. Sit back and let Jerry entertain you." – Marshall J. Cook, author, teacher, and editor, *Extra Innings*

Hyper Fiction: 50 stories for people in a hurry – Book 3 . . . "Like a box of mixed chocolates, master storyteller Jerry Peterson's *Hyper Fiction 3* provides delectable short stories sure to please and surprise." –

Bill Mathis, author, *The Rooming House Diaries, The Rooming House Gallery, Face Your Fears*

ABOUT THE AUTHOR

I write crime novels and short stories set in Kansas, Tennessee, and Wisconsin.

Before becoming a writer, I taught speech, English, and theater in Wisconsin high schools, then worked in communications for farm organizations for a decade in Wisconsin, Michigan, Kansas, and Colorado.

I followed that with a decade as a reporter, photographer, and editor for newspapers in Colorado, West Virginia, Virginia, and Tennessee.

Today, I'm back home and writing in Wisconsin, the land of dairy cows, craft beer, and really good books.

COMING SOON

Night Flight, the third book in my Wings Over the
Mountains series of novels.